Steel Defender

Rusted Wasteland

Book 2

Cameron Coral

Edited by Lori Diederich

Cover by Roy Migabon

9 8 7 6 5 4 3 2 1

2nd edition, March 2024

Stay updated on Cameron's books by signing up for the Cameron Coral Reading List:
CameronCoral.com/sign-up

You'll be added to my reading list, and I'll send you a digital copy of *CROSSING THE VOID: A Space Opera Science-Fiction Short Story* to say thank you.

Contents

Part One
Hemlock

Chapter 1
Not all robots

Block enjoyed a gritty, grimy baseboard. The point where floor met wall collected the most dust and filth, especially when the dirt-encrusted boots of soldiers were constantly stomping around. Black sediment collected in the crevices and cracks—remnants of shoe grease, soil, glass bits, and sharp pebbles. Though baseboards were often overlooked, Block made sure to keep them clean. He ran the edge of his mop along the corridor in the neglected former elementary school that now served as Hemlock's command station.

Block tried his best to keep the olive green linoleum floors polished, but it was tough. Nova had told him to stay out of their way—out of everybody's way—which was challenging because men and women came in and out of the gymnasium at all times of the day. At first, the human soldiers had been frightened of Block's presence, recoiling from him or casting narrow-eyed looks while muttering slurs. They called him things like Rust Bucket, Scrapper, and Sheetmetal. Those were the nicer names.

Until one day Nova gathered them all together and

told them Block was a friendly robot, that she vouched for him, and that he'd saved her life. Nova was Shane's girlfriend, so they looked up to her. They had to. Shane was in charge of the Hemlock survivor camp.

The soldiers were actually soldiers-in-training, people who had survived the SoldierBot raids on cities. Any women and men in decent shape between the ages of sixteen and sixty-five trained for combat and defense. There was no choice after the AI Uprising.

The troops relaxed a bit after her speech. They stared Block down and smirked. The name calling didn't stop, but they were less obvious about it. And then, after a few weeks of such treatment, they'd let their guard down and just ignored him. That was fine with Block. He didn't like to be the center of attention anyway.

Sunlight filtered in and cast a speckled glare on a yellowing concrete wall. Dust motes drifted through the air, rendered brilliant in the sunbeam's arc.

"That won't do." He whipped out his vacuum extension—a long hose through which he sucked in particles that fed into his microbial fuel cell chamber. There, his digestive enzymes devoured dirt, grime, oils, and petroleum, fueling his mechanical body. Block strolled forward, still unsteady on his modified feet. He'd lost his original sole, heel, and ankle parts three months ago when Cybel Venatrix had fired upon his legs. That had been the second worst day of his life.

Strangely—and Block had contemplated this many times—it had also been the second *best* day of his life because Wally and Nova had been kept safe. Alive. That a day could be both awful and joyful didn't compute in his logic module. He couldn't explain it, and there were no other robots around to discuss it with.

He walked down the narrow corridor, noting the sagging ceiling tiles—very grimy! He added them to his cleaning checklist for later. Extending the mouth of the vacuum before him, he sucked in dust, weaving the hose back and forth as if conducting an orchestra. The floating specks first spread, then clustered together as if finding protection in staying close to one another. Block was like a dust predator, sucking them in, feasting on them.

He supposed there was something interesting in this chain of events. A lot of skin particles fell off of humans—over a million cells every day. He sucked in their leavings and used the human bits to feed himself. Nothing was wasted. He was helping, in his way, even if nobody realized it.

A gruff voice came from behind. "Move it."

Block had stepped into the middle of the hallway, lost in the frenzy of dust collection. He spun quickly and was nearly knocked over as Shane brushed past him.

If Block could physically cringe, he would have. Shane was the one person Nova had especially warned him to steer clear of. Block backed against the wall, pointing his vacuum tube down. He even turned the suction off.

Nova walked a few feet behind Shane and lingered after he kept going. She held a thermos in her hand from which little wisps of steam rose. "Hey, Block," she said, half smiling.

"Hi. I tried to stay out of his way, but he came upon me so fast."

"I know. He's just..." She sighed, arched her head back, then rolled it around on her neck. Block had only seen her do that when she was exhausted.

"Are you having trouble sleeping again?"

She nodded.

"You could come by this evening, and I'll help if you would like." When he'd worked at The Drake hotel in Chicago, Block had learned to manipulate certain pressure points that helped people relax. He hadn't been allowed to practice on the hotel guests, but he'd helped the human employees often. Twice before, he'd helped Nova fall asleep by pressing points on her spine and neck.

She looked sideways in the direction Shane had gone. "I don't think that's such a good idea right now." She sipped her hot drink and strode toward the gymnasium.

"Okay." Block tucked away his vacuum hose, grasped the handle of the broom, and started pushing it along the baseboard edges. Then he stopped, remembering something. "Nova?"

She turned back.

In his second to lowest voice setting, barely audible, he asked, "May I visit?"

She frowned. "Also not a good idea." She moved closer, confiding in him. "Shane's been in a foul mood. Things aren't going well. Now isn't a great time."

"I see."

Block had only visited Wally twice in the five months he'd been at the Hemlock camp in Colorado. The child was in good care. That much he knew. She lived with a woman named Helen who had lost her young son in the fighting between AI and humans. But Shane didn't like Block to have any interaction with Wally. Nova had explained that, according to Shane, a robot and human relationship was unnatural. Shane—and most humans—harbored resentment and fear against robots since the supercomputer Mach X had overtaken the world's computer systems, caused the AI Uprising, and declared war on humans.

The humans had reason to be suspicious. After the Uprising, many robots had become unpredictable. He'd witnessed SoldierBots execute his former boss and fifty hotel guests.

Still, not all robots were dangerous.

Block hung his head and pushed the mop a few inches. He stepped forward, his cobbled-together soles awkwardly clanking against the linoleum. Nova had welded them herself from scavenged metal from rust-speckled pupil desks, claiming they were temporary until they could find stronger material.

A tattered old bulletin board hung on the wall. The red construction paper background had faded to a dull pink. Most of the children's decorations had been torn down, but one remained: a child's handprint, stamped in yellow paint. Block paused and stared at it, then reached out his hand and placed his steel digits on top. His was much larger than the small child's print, of course.

He wished there were more tiny humans around. They weren't as frightened of him as the adults.

He began mopping, but Nova came over and touched his arm. "Five minutes," she whispered. "But we have to be quick and avoid anyone seeing us."

Five minutes with Wally didn't seem like much at all, but he could play back the memory as often as he wanted. Maybe if he was quiet and polite, Nova could finally convince Shane to let him spend time with Wally. Humans changed their views on occasion. It was rare, but it happened.

But would Shane ever believe that robots and humans could be friends?

Chapter 2
Who's there?

Block followed Nova outside into the daylight, adjusting his visual sensors to account for the bright rays that slowly warmed the surrounding forest. The school stood in a grassy clearing, and in the woods, among a shelter of trees, the camp's occupants sheltered in tents. There were a few camper vans and small trailers that housed families with children, elderly, and sick people who needed more warmth than a nylon tent and sleeping bags could provide. The treetops provided coverage in case aerial drones passed over. One of the Hemlock engineers had figured out how to broadcast a jamming signal which effectively cast a dead zone around the camp. Any drones surveying the countryside would bypass the area. The camp had been spared from attacks by Mach X's forces.

It was morning, and a few people surrounded small campfires. They cooked food or heated up water to wash clothes and fill the makeshift showers. Every able-bodied person at Hemlock had a job. Life at the camp differed from The Drake. There, humans had experienced every convenience—electricity, instant hot water, hundreds of channels of entertainment television, phones, and gadgets. But after the Uprising, life had changed drastically. Millions of lives had been lost in the fighting. Mach X's forces had overtaken the large cities, leaving people to scramble for refuge. Hemlock was just one of many human survivor camps across the former U.S. Shane's military background meant he could assemble and train fighters to defend themselves.

There were no luxuries at camp. The elementary school had no power. Water was heated by fire. A few scavenged generators fed the equipment they used: offline computers and radios to communicate with other human rebel camps.

Gone were the connected devices that hooked everyone up to MachNet, the communications network that had been created by Mach X and later manipulated to lock humans out and topple their infrastructure. People now communicated via walkie-talkie devices. "Good, old-fashioned tech," Nova called it.

Block was the only robot intelligence at camp, and Shane only tolerated him because Nova insisted on it. Block would have been scrapped for his metal and Central Processing Unit if Shane had his way.

Nova and Block discreetly traveled a winding side path that veered away from the main gathering area where most people were cooking and going about their daily chores. After a minute, they ended up behind Helen's trailer.

"Stay here." Nova rounded the corner and rapped on the front door. After half a minute, she appeared and jerked her head. "Come on. Quickly."

Block followed her up two small steps into the camper

trailer where Helen and Wally lived. Nova shut the door behind them.

Helen sat beside Wally on the bed. The little girl was just over a year old and had changed in the scant two months since Block had last seen her.

Her face lit up when she saw him. "Bock!" she said and reached out her arms.

But Block hesitated. He glanced at Nova, waiting for permission. If he angered Nova, he was in trouble.

"Go on." She nodded.

"Hello, Helen," he said.

Helen smoothed back her wavy red hair and arched a lone, dark eyebrow. She lifted Wally down to the floor, which caused the toddler to squeal, "Wheeee!" Dressed in a yellow T-shirt and pink pants, her plump little legs wobbled as she raced over, stumbled, then crawled to Block and wrapped her arms around his leg, pulling herself up to stand.

"Hello, little Wally." Block bent over to look at her.

"Bock, bock." She giggled.

Helen fidgeted, seeming nervous.

"We'll be gone in just a few minutes," Nova said. "He really wanted to see her."

"Sure." Helen kept her eyes glued on Wally.

Nova tugged the shade and glanced out the window.

Block gently peeled Wally's arms from his leg and lowered himself down to kneel on the floor. The hydraulics behind his knees let out a small hiss.

Wally bobbed up and down, then leaned into his chest for a closer hug. Block wrapped his arms around her, noting her weight had increased by 2.3 pounds. He still accessed the log he'd kept of her weight, height and fecal matter from when they had traveled together. He supposed he didn't really need to keep Wally's log, but he enjoyed reviewing it from time to time.

"Ba wub you," Wally said.

"Wow, she really wants to talk," Nova said.

"What does that mean? What's wub?" Block asked.

"Love," Nova said, enunciating. "Little ones can't pronounce words as well, so you have to try to decipher."

Wally *loved* him? Nobody had ever said that to Block before. He didn't even know how to respond. Nothing in his etiquette modules or housekeeping programming had ever trained him for such an event.

Wally pulled away, looked at Block, then curled one hand into a chubby fist. She knocked on his chest plate. "Knock, ock."

"That's my torso. Tor-so," he enunciated for her edification.

Nova burst out laughing. "You're supposed to say, 'Who's there?'"

Block was not computing. "Who is supposed to say that? Me?" He looked at Wally. "Who's there?"

"My kack, bye-ba." He didn't understand one word of what she was saying.

Helen came over and crouched, smoothing back wisps of light brown hair sticking up from Wally's head. "We're just starting to learn knock-knock jokes."

"Knock knock?" Block said. He would have to research the strange human expression later. Then he remembered the little gift he had for Wally. He opened his thigh compartment and removed the odd-looking square with the many colored tiles. "I have something for you." He hid the cube inside his palms and then offered it to Wally.

She squealed and tried to open his palms with her

soft, tiny little fingers. After five seconds, Block relented and revealed the object.

Wally stared at the cube, then grinned, looking up at Block.

"A Rubik's Cube!" Nova said. "I haven't seen one of those in ages. Where'd you find it?"

"In the school," Block said. "I was cleaning out an old desk and happened across it. I thought Wally might like it."

"How does it work?" Helen asked.

"See, all the colors are scattered," Nova said while Wally grabbed the cube, shook it, and pointed at the tiles. "You're supposed to move all the same colors onto one side, on each side. It's actually really hard."

Wally furrowed her brows and studied the cube. She continued to poke at the tiles.

"She really seems to like it, Block. Good job," Nova said.

"Thank you. I'll try to find more little presents."

The trailer sank a few inches as someone climbed the stairs, then banged on the door. "Nova? Are you in there?"

It was Shane.

Chapter 3
Ignorant little foot soldiers

Nova motioned for Block and Helen to quiet before she opened the trailer door a crack. "Hey. Just visiting with Helen. You need something?"

"Is that robot with you again?" Shane asked. "I told you..."

Nova shifted her legs in the doorway. "Listen, I know you're angry that Block won't answer your—" But he pushed past her, shoved the door open, and stood in the doorway with bent head, his shock of dark red hair adding another inch to his six-foot-four frame.

"I knew it." Shane glared at her, his left eye twitching above the deep scar on his upper cheek. "I gave you another chance, but I said if you brought the robot here, I'd lock the thing back up in a cell. Get it out of here."

Nova clenched her fists. "He's not bothering anyone."

"Are you kidding me? The bot is offending everyone in this camp. Every time you drag it out, you're hurting every person who lost someone in the war."

"I took him around the back, away from the others."

"That doesn't matter." He lowered his voice a few

notes. "Everyone still saw you. How do you think I found out? Someone came and told me what you were up to."

Nova's voice got that grainy edge to it like when she was angry. "You said you trusted me. What, do you have your soldiers follow me?"

Shane clenched his jaw, then glared at Helen. "Do not allow the baby to see the robot. Understand? That's an order."

Helen grabbed Wally and held her close.

"It needs to stay in the school, out of sight, like I told you, Nova." He spun and stormed off.

Block returned to the school after the fiasco. Nova accompanied him, holding her chin high as they walked past two young men and two women loitering by the school's side entrance, smoking cigarettes and chatting. Block's offensive odor register clicked on, warning him of the toxic fumes, but he didn't dare say anything to them. Nova was agitated, her gait stiff as they approached. The soldiers-in-training fell silent as soon as Block and Nova came into view. As they reached the door, Nova whirled and faced the group.

"Hey, Pete." She'd mentioned him before; he was Shane's protégé. "What have you been up to today?" Her voice was deeper than usual.

Pete, who had been leaning casually against the brick wall straightened. "Not much. How are you?"

She folded her arms and widened her stance. "Not so great. Turns out some rat-face is going around spying on me and reporting to Shane."

His smile vanished. "Uh..."

Nova smirked. "I got to thinking, who would do such a thing? I ran through all the potential people in my head.

Thought back to all the people I'd seen this morning. And the weird thing is, I kept coming back to you."

His cheeks turned a shade of sunset. "I didn't mean to—"

"Save it." Nova came forward and jabbed a finger against his chest. "Don't tell me you're just doing your job or looking out for Shane, because that's a load of crap. You stay out of my business." She had him pinned against the wall. The others backed away slowly.

"Why do you help that thing?" Pete asked, glancing at Block. "One of those things killed my brother."

Nova relented and stepped back. "I'm sorry that happened, but I can assure you this kind of robot did not hurt your brother or any other human. He's just a CleanerBot."

"It doesn't matter." He spit onto the soil near his feet. "They're all the same. Enemies."

Nova glared at him, then looked at the others who avoided her gaze. "Get back to work." She opened the door and motioned for Block to go inside. They traveled the hallway, Block keeping close to the wall. They had to round a corner and pass the gymnasium which was the highest chance to run into Shane.

Beside him, Nova huffed. "God, they irritate me. Spying on me like that. And Shane does nothing to educate his ignorant little foot soldiers."

Block couldn't process a reply. Instead, he focused on his shoddy feet, noting the loud metal clang as they struck the linoleum.

As they passed the gym's open door, Block spotted Shane leaning over a table, studying something on a large piece of paper and rubbing his thick beard. They passed without notice, and Nova continued on with him, which he hadn't anticipated.

"I'm returning to my quarters," he said. "You don't have to accompany me. I know the way."

"I know," she blurted out, but she kept walking. "I'm just irritated. Need to blow off some steam. If I see Shane right now, I'll say something that I'll regret."

"I haven't finished my cleaning duties for today."

"Take the day off," she said. "It's better if you're not seen today."

What was a day off? Block had never experienced one before. He knew humans went on vacation. Even Mr. Wallace, the hard-working hotel manager at The Drake, had once departed on a five-day vacation. But robots didn't need days off. He sensed Nova thought she was doing him a favor, but he wasn't sure how to pass the time.

They traveled the familiar hallway, passing the porcelain drinking fountain. This section of the school, where Hemlock used two small classrooms as storage for weapons and other scavenged supplies, was the least occupied. Block ran his fingertips along the top of a shelf that featured tiny coat hooks underneath at a height perfect for small children. An old, tattered sign at the end of the hallway read: First Graders. At the end of the hall was the entrance to the basement where Block lived.

Upon reaching his door, Nova hesitated. "What are you going to do today?"

"I don't know."

She looked around at the empty hallway and shrugged. "Well, I suppose you could clean around here. But just this hallway and the classrooms in it. Don't go beyond."

Block nodded.

"You have nothing to occupy you?" she asked. "Do you want some books?"

"I have read every book in the school."

Her jaw dropped. "*Every* book?"

"Yes. Reading occupies my time at night. But I have read and memorized all of them. Mostly there were children's books."

"I see." She shoved her hands in her jean pockets. "Which one was your favorite? I could use a good read right now."

"I enjoyed one called *James and the Giant Peach*. I think you will like that one."

"Giant peach? What's it about?" Her eyes narrowed, and her suspicion was clear.

"A young boy's parents are killed tragically in a zoo accident, and he is sent to live with his two aunts. They are terrible, mean people. He discovers a magical peach which grows to an enormous size. He finds a way inside where he meets interesting creatures and has adventures."

"A magical peach?" She smirked. "Now I get why you're bored."

"Bored? As in boredom? That is a human emotion I don't experience."

"Then you're lucky. We humans get bored with a lot of things, partners included." She rolled her eyes.

"What are you planning to do today?" Block asked.

"Some soldiers set up a punching bag in one of the classrooms. I'm going to go pretend it's Shane for a little while."

"But that means you would hit the bag. You would punch Shane?"

"Metaphorically."

"Why would you want to conduct an act of violence on Shane?"

"Don't you?" she asked, her eyebrows arching. "With the way he treats you?"

"I don't want to hurt anyone or anything."

"Shane believes that we have to do things we don't want as a way to survive."

"I wish he would realize that I'm harmless and let me visit Wally."

Nova chewed on her lip. "If you would answer his questions—"

"His questions are all about how robots work, their weak spots—all things that will let Shane and his troops kill more robots."

"Sorry. I wish there was another way. I'll keep working on him, when he's not in such a foul mood. I better get going."

Block watched as Nova walked away, realizing she was his only friend at Hemlock—and perhaps in the entire world, other than Wally. But the baby was in a whole different category than any other human. Wally was family.

Block opened the basement door and descended the narrow spiral staircase. He gripped the banister carefully because of his uneven soles. Taking a tumble in the basement all by himself would not be good.

He had nothing left to read, and he'd devoured all of his stored media shows fifty-seven times already. He sat down on a chair, a hard plastic one designed for children and small for his frame. Still, it was the only place to sit in the basement, and it's where he passed the time.

He considered Nova and processed the events of the day, replaying them in his memory cloud just to be sure he didn't miss some important detail. He fast-forwarded to the part where Shane entered the trailer. Nova and Shane had been angry at each other. Anger was a human emotion that Block could easily detect—their faces grew red, voices got loud, and they frowned. Humans got angry with each other a lot, sometimes over small things. Often, Block couldn't even understand the root cause of the conflict like when Nova had gotten mad at the soldier named Pete. She'd accused him of spying on her. Block supposed that would be annoying. He was glad there was nobody spying on him, but then he wondered if perhaps there was someone, but he just didn't realize it. He would have to ask Nova about that later.

She was the only person he trusted at Hemlock—the only person who even talked to him outside of Helen. And that was only because Nova brought him to visit Wally occasionally. Shane grumbled and told him to get out of the way. The soldiers mocked him or treated him like he didn't exist.

He didn't want to have to rely on Nova, but there was no other choice. She seemed to be the only one who would protect him. She was the soldier who had led a sniper attack over a year ago when Block had first discovered Wally in an abandoned school in Iowa. She'd been the shooter who had terminated a SoldierBot and could have fired at Block too. For that reason alone, he shouldn't have trusted her. Worse yet, she'd only admitted it when he'd confronted her about it.

Block backtracked even further in his memory cloud and replayed his early memories of Wally—when he'd cared for her in the attack's aftermath. He'd found a little house and later traveled to an AI market where he tried to find water and food. It had been five months, and yet

Block often replayed the memories of his time with Wally.

He fast forwarded again to an event he didn't like to re-watch—when he'd faced Cybel Venatrix in a standoff. Before shooting him, she'd said something curious about Wally. A statement he'd replayed over and over, yet it didn't fully compute. She'd said Mach X had implanted his consciousness into Wally. Block had told no one about Wally's secret, not even Nova.

How could a machine intelligence insert its consciousness into a human?

A child?

Even Block knew human brains didn't work like that. Or did they? Had Mach X discovered some new innovation?

If so, what did it mean for Wally?

Chapter 4
Risk of collapse high

The next morning, Block left the basement at 0500 and ventured out into the first grade hallway. Just before sunrise was his favorite time of day because hardly any soldiers were up and about so early. Most of them didn't rise until well after 0600. He stepped carefully so as not to make a racket with his feet and wake anyone who might be sleeping inside the school. Armed with his mop and bucket, he headed for the gymnasium. He was careful when cleaning it because he had to stay out of Shane's way. That meant getting in and out very early, before Shane arrived.

He approached the gym door cautiously. Only two soldiers were inside, finishing their night shift—Shelly and Cara. They were less hostile to him than the others, so he stepped in, pushing the mop bucket. The two women glanced at him, then went back to whatever they were doing on their computer screens. Without a word, he began to swipe the mop along the floor, addressing the corners and baseboards.

Static crackled from a radio. Shelly rose from her seat, walked over to the transceiver, and spoke into a microphone. "Hemlock Command Station. Go ahead."

A voice filtered through the speaker. "Hemlock, this is Magnolia. We are under—" Static overtook the channel.

Shelly spoke into the mic again. "Magnolia, say again? Hemlock is here. Over."

Seconds ticked by as more static poured through the airwaves, punctuated with a high-pitched chirping. Finally, the man's voice said, "Magnolia here. Emergency emergency. We are under attack. Forces moving west. Over."

Shelly's eyes grew wide, and Cara bolted up from her seat.

"Magnolia," Shelly said, "report on your situation. Do you require support?"

More chirping and static, then the man replied, "Negative. It's too late. Our command center is down to a handful of people. We're making a last stand, but their numbers are too big."

The two women stared at each other. Block paused his mopping, not wanting to make a sound.

The man's voice carried through once more. "Look out for your camp. When the machines come, their numbers are strong. You must help your people. Get them out. They knew our location even though we were jamming their signals. We tried to stop them..." His voice became garbled. More static spewed forth, then it sounded like the radio on his end had fallen from a great height. And then nothing but dead static.

Shelly set the microphone down. "Go get Pete. We need to wake Commander Shane."

Cara ran out of the room. Shelly placed her palms on the table, swaying. Then she looked at Block and clenched her jaw. "Get out." Her cheeks reddened.

Block wasted no time. He set the mop back into the bucket and wheeled it out, exiting the gymnasium ahead of Shane and others arriving. Walking faster this time, he knew to keep out of sight. This was a disaster. Mach X's forces had found the Magnolia camp's location. That meant Hemlock was in danger. Even with the jamming device, they might be discovered.

And once the SoldierBots found Block, they would know Wally was close. No doubt, Mach X still searched for her.

He returned to the basement, his logic module indicating it was the safest place to process the confusing events. He paced across the floor—a behavior he'd picked up from humans. Then he chased down cobwebs that had sprung up since his last cleaning. In a far corner, several pebbles had rolled onto the ground. He hadn't noticed them before and scooped them up through his vacuum hose. Part of the wall paneling had peeled open at the bottom. Odd. He accessed his memory cloud and compared it to what he'd seen before. The wall panel had definitely changed. He scanned it, discovering that the plaster was damp and that water was entering the basement somehow, damaging the wall. He supposed he should fix the leak, wherever it was coming from, so he inserted his steel fingers behind the panel and removed it. It was a wide three-by-three-foot panel. It came off easily, and he set it aside. A small puddle of water had collected on the floor, coming from a place deeper in the building's foundation, but there was something else—an opening behind the wall panel that led farther inside. Block peered inside, relying on his night vision to illuminate a tunnel that measured four feet tall by three wide.

Threat level assessment: 7.3 of 10.

There could be many dangers inside the tunnel. His processor flashed through 736 scenarios in seconds. The worst-case would be the tunnel rupturing and caving in, trapping him inside. But he knew Nova would come looking for him, eventually. She would enter the basement and see the missing wall panel.

He didn't want to be injured again. The experience had been awful. Yet, what if the tunnel proved useful in getting Wally and the others to safety?

Block decided the risk was worth knowing where the tunnel led. While he explored it, he would map out the spatial dimensions in case it proved useful to Nova. He had to bend over and walk in a crouch since the tunnel was only four feet tall.

His humidity reading increased by five percent inside the damp tunnel. The temperature had dropped from the basement's consistent sixty-two degrees Fahrenheit to fifty-nine. Block commanded his programming to ignore the massive spiderwebs, patches of mold, and sediment on the ground. It would take him a week to clean this tunnel! There wouldn't be time if the SoldierBots were on their way. Block had once watched a movie with Mr. Wallace called *The Shawshank Redemption.* The hero had escaped through a hole he'd carved into the wall of his prison cell. He used it to escape and flee the prison forever. Block wondered whether he could escape from Hemlock using this tunnel. Shane didn't want him around, anyway, but he couldn't leave Wally behind. Escaping alone was out of the question.

Block followed as the tunnel curved slightly. Water trickled along the ground as he calculated he was 138 feet from the basement entrance. Why would a school have such a tunnel? Did humans often dig tunnels? He'd have to ask Nova about that. She would know. She had an answer for everything.

He plodded through the tunnel and gradually noticed the walls were deteriorating the farther he got. Piles of rubble had collected on the ground.

Threat level assessment: 8.6 of 10. Risk of collapse high.

But he'd come so far and spied a sharp turn only fifteen feet away. He walked on, looked around the corner, and spotted a dead end. A ladder was bolted into the wall. Beams of daylight filtered into the tunnel from an opening above. He shuffled forward, grasped the ladder, and shook to see if it was steady. It was. Above his head, a metal grate led to an exit. He climbed the ladder, his shoddy heels slipping against the rusty metal rungs. His palms clanked against the metal, and reaching the top, he pressed against the grate. It was heavy, but he pushed and slid it off to one side. Poking his head above ground, he spied grass and a large bush that sheltered the tunnel hatch. There was nobody around, and he emerged from the hole onto a hilltop, unsure of his location. He spun, walked ten feet beyond the bush, and spotted the elementary school down the hill. The tunnel had ended up outside the Hemlock perimeter! To his back was dense forest. No sign of paths carved by humans or animals. The woods with their thick treetops would provide good shelter for an escape and cover against drone surveillance. This was promising. He would return to the school and alert Nova about his discovery. They could hide the people in the camp and have an escape route when Mach X's forces came.

Nova would be grateful for the information. And maybe Shane would begin to trust Block more.

Chapter 5
It does the cleaning

On the return trip, Block remapped the tunnel, noting the gradations, exact width and height, and the weakest points of the tunnel—information Nova would be interested in. If they were going to hide all of the occupants of the camp, it was worth noting which parts had the most danger of collapsing. By now Shane, Nova, and the other troops would be planning for the impending attack. Everybody at camp would be on high alert. Perhaps, the civilians were already packing up their tents and things. He wished he could go straight away to check on Wally, but that would land him in trouble.

Back in the safety of the basement, he detached a polishing arm and dusted off the grime and particles that had collected on him inside the tunnel. Then he climbed the spiral stairs, jogged through the first grade hallway, rounded two corners, and halted near the gymnasium. Two armed soldiers stood guard. Cara and Shelly approached from the opposite direction, Nova by their side. She listened as the two women talked.

"Then his voice cut out, and there was a really loud noise," Shelly said. "And then it was just static."

Nova glanced at Block and frowned. She told the women to head inside, then jogged over. "What are you doing here?"

"I have important information."

"This is literally the worst possible time," she said, raising her hands for emphasis. "There's going to be an attack."

"I know. I was there when the message came in over the radio."

She recoiled. "You were? Shelly and Cara didn't mention that."

"I'm good at being invisible."

"Look, I don't have time for this. The camp is on red alert. We're bracing for an attack and starting to mount a defense." She started walking backward. "Go to the basement and just lay low. I'll come look for you."

"Wait. Please. I found something." But it was too late. She was already inside the gymnasium. He stepped forward and glimpsed Shane talking to a group of people. Nova joined the cluster. Pete was there, along with Shelly and Cara.

He needed to tell them. If he retreated to the basement, he would be alone and nobody would know anything about the tunnel. Why hadn't Nova just listened to him?

He studied the two guards stationed by the gym-turned-command-center doors. The young man on the left wore an olive green military jacket and a black cap. Block didn't recognize him. He'd seen the woman around the campfires on one of his trips to visit Wally. She had curly brown hair tied back into a ponytail. She clenched her teeth as she eyed Block, her hands trembling slightly.

He needed to get Nova's attention again. He stepped forward. "Hello. I have an important message for Nova."

The man clutched his rifle and pointed it at Block. "Halt where you are."

The female guard stepped over and touched the man's shoulder. "Jake, that's the robot I was telling you about. It does the cleaning."

"Hello," Block repeated. "I don't mean to cause trouble. I just need to talk to Nova. Can you please tell her I'm here?" Then he realized she would probably ignore him. "Or rather, can you please tell her I have important information that will help against the attack?"

The woman's eyes narrowed. "What do you know about the attack? That's classified information."

"I was here when the radio communication came through at 0521 this morning."

The two guards looked at each other, confusion dashed across their faces.

It was then that Shane came out of the gym and flinched as soon as he saw Block. "What the—? Hey, Nova," he shouted over his shoulder. "Come here."

She darted over and furrowed her brow at Block.

"I told you to keep that thing away," he said to her, hands on his hips.

She stepped into the middle of the hallway between Block and the soldiers, pushing the man's gun barrel to point at the floor. "Stop aiming at him. He's on our side. I *did* tell him to stay in the basement." She looked at Shane. "I'll take care of it."

"See that you do." Shane walked away.

"Wait," Block said. "I have important information that will help against the attack."

Shane spun on his heels, then stomped over to Block, close enough that Block stepped back. "Are the Soldier-Bots communicating with you? Are you telling them our camp's location?"

Block shook his head from side to side and raised his hands. "No. Nothing like that. I want to protect the camp."

"He does." Nova glared at Shane. "That's the truth. He wants to keep the girl safe."

Cara ran out of the gym. "Sir." She held a walkie-talkie in her hand. "Where should the men position the missile launchers?"

Shane grunted. "I want them spaced out on the perimeter. Tell the team to pepper bombs out on the road, leading in. I want snipers on the roof and at the forest's edge. We'll destroy every last one of them."

"Yes, sir." Cara ran back inside, chattering away on the comm.

"What about my idea?" Nova asked.

"I know you're trying to help," Shane said, "but trying to negotiate with them is pointless. Have you ever heard of the machines negotiating with any of the other rebel camps?"

"No, I suppose not. But isn't it worth trying?"

"And what do we have to offer?" Shane asked. "Hey SoldierBots, let's make peace with each other? Maybe we should offer up our weapons so they can slaughter us more easily?"

Nova grimaced. "We're risking the lives of everyone at this camp. We'll be outnumbered, outmatched."

Block knew she was right. The SoldierBots had Mechs, advanced armor, and artillery.

"We've been over this," Shane said. "There is no negotiation. Unless, that is, you want to offer up Wally?" He paused. "We destroy every single machine we can."

Pete, lingering in the doorway, spoke up. "What if we could give them that CleanerBot? Maybe it could talk to them?"

Nova clenched her fists. "Don't even think about it. Block has earned his way to be here, even if you don't think so. He saved my life, and he saved Wally's life. He's not a SoldierBot."

"Well, they wanted him before," Pete said.

Shane rubbed his beard in thought. "All options are on the table at this point."

Being handed over to the SoldierBots? This wasn't the way Block had expected things to go. His scenario processor kicked in. He processed 398 scenarios, and in seventy-seven percent of them, Shane handed him over to the enemy. Worst of all, everyone in the camp died when the SoldierBots dropped bombs on the school and the surrounding forest. In 99.25 percent of the scenarios, Wally perished. He could not let that happen.

Shane sighed, folded his arms, and glared at Block. "What information do you have?"

A new scenario emerged, one he decided was the best option. Block needed a diversion, and fast. "I know something you can do to confuse the drones."

Chapter 6
We want the code

The worst-case scenario was unfolding. Shane knew Wally was important to Mach X, though he didn't know exactly why. Would he use her as a bargaining chip? He'd admitted being open to the possibility of handing her over. If that happened, Block would never see her again. Worse, she could be harmed. As his logic processor ran through thousands of scenarios, he kept coming back to the one that seemed the simplest, with the highest odds of success. He would take Wally and leave through the tunnel before Mach X's forces arrived. All he wanted was to protect her and let her grow up as a normal girl. That would never happen if Mach X got ahold of her.

Telling Shane and Nova about the tunnel was no longer an option, so instead he told them about a glitch in the aerial drone's design. They could beam out a code patch, which was actually a virus that Block would help them create. The malicious code would jam their geo-positioning coordinates, rendering them blind.

Shane cursed when Block revealed the plan. He stomped over and thrust his index finger into Block's face plate. "You knew about this all along! You could've told us. The other camps would have had a chance."

It was true. Months ago, Nova had begged Block for information about Mach X's forces, but Block had resisted, not wanting to fuel the fighting, hoping peace would eventually prevail and life could go back to normal. Now, he wondered if such a thing would ever be possible.

Block backed away from Shane who was ready to erupt like a volcanic rift. Nova rested a hand on Shane's back. "It doesn't matter. We have the intelligence now, and we need to use it."

But Shane glared at Block, breath ragged and chest heaving. "What else is that thing hiding from us?"

Nova stared at Block. "If there's anything else you can tell us that will be helpful... say it now."

Block looked between Shane and Nova. "That is all I can think of right now. They travel with combat Mechs, which you know." He remembered the Mech Unit who'd threatened the barricade at the New Denver checkpoint.

"Thank you, Block. We want the code you offered." Nova took Shane's hand, whispering in his ear, and the two headed into the gym.

Block followed them inside, the two guards begrudgingly letting him pass. Once inside, he used one of the computer terminals to compose the strings of code that would sabotage the drones. Nova hovered nearby, watching while Shane stood at a high table, studying maps with Pete and the other soldiers.

"Will this really work?" Nova asked quietly.

"I'm not sure. There is a forty-seven percent probability of success."

"I'll take it." The hollows under her eyes told Block she hadn't slept again.

While he worked on the virus code, he calculated what supplies he would need for his escape: food, water, diapers, blankets for warmth... the list went on. These were all things he could secure, but he would need to be stealthy. The hardest part would be retrieving Wally. Helen rarely left her side, and now that the camp was on alert, she would be even more vigilant.

"This will take me twenty-seven minutes."

"Right." She stretched her arms behind her back, stifling a yawn. "I'm going to grab some coffee and check on the others. Will you be okay here by yourself?"

He looked sideways as he typed. Her eyes were slightly narrowed, but in a way that did not reveal anger. He couldn't calculate her emotion. "I will be fine." He went back to studying the screen before him as codes of black and green letters arched across the screen, fluttering by as his fingers typed a rapid beat on the plastic keyboard.

Nova sighed. "Thank you for helping us. I should have let you be around people more—visit with Wally." She hesitated, standing there, and Block didn't know what to say. Her mouth twisted like she wanted to keep talking, but then she walked away.

While the others were distracted, Block attempted to open the encrypted file from Incubator X79. It was his 547th attempt. He was able to simultaneously process both the coding exercise and the file retrieval, but he couldn't do much else. He'd nearly reached full processing capacity. That meant he could no longer plan Wally's escape. Still, he knew there was something important in those files.

He played with a string of code and tried bit shifting, creating a circle out of the bit values, hoping that would break the barrier. But it was built with logic he couldn't crack.

Files encrypted. Access attempt unsuccessful, the text flashed in his internal feed.

He went back to programming the virus.

Nova returned once Block had finished creating the drone virus. Shane watched them from across the room.

"I can't thank you enough for this," she said. "Shane's grateful too, but... He won't show it. He doesn't want to lose face in front of the others."

"Lose face?" Block had never heard such a term.

The worry lines around her mouth relaxed a bit. "It means if he starts treating you nicely now, he'll look bad to the others. It will show he was wrong. Do you understand?"

"Yes. I think so. I am done here."

She hesitated. "Is there anything else you can do to help us prepare for the attack? Something we're not thinking of? You really surprised me with this drone virus thing." She leaned against the high table where the monitor rested. "I had no idea you were capable of programming. I thought you just mopped floors."

"I suppose I should have mentioned it, but no one asked."

"Fair point. Right now, we need all the help we can get. Everyone here at camp is in danger." She frowned. "Wally is in danger. What else can you do to protect the camp?"

The tunnel. Everyone could escape. Yet, if he revealed its existence, his own escape plans would be spoiled.

"I cannot think of anything else." This was true, sort of. All his processing power was focused on how to get Wally out safely.

"Okay. Thanks again for the help with the drones. It's going to be a huge advantage."

"You're welcome. I'm going back to cleaning now. Is that fine by you?"

"Cleaning? Now?" She opened her mouth as if to speak, but then hesitated. "I guess so. If that's how you want to spend your time."

"Yes. Goodbye." He walked away, leaving the gym behind, not sparing a glance at Nova.

Back in the first grade hallway, he entered the supply classroom. There he found a backpack and shoved cans of food inside—macaroni and cheese, ravioli, green beans, and sweet potatoes. According to his memory files, these were all foods palatable to Wally. Water was high on the list yet nowhere in sight. He would have to get into the supply room next to the canteen where they kept the water rations. The soldiers received the best supply from scavenged water bottles and tins. Everyone else in camp drank from well water that they boiled. Helen would have diapers in her trailer. He could grab enough to last for several days and later restock. There was no telling how long he and Wally would have to fend for themselves and keep to the forest. Days probably.

The hardest part of his plan was retrieving Wally. His logic processor played out 112 scenarios. The best time to take her would be after dark. He could dress in soldier clothing and a cap so he'd be less noticeable. Getting around the guards would be the hardest part. If they discovered him in human clothing, they would be suspicious. Dangerous. The shifts changed out at 2305 hours. But now, with attack imminent, the usual routines were in jeopardy.

Could he somehow lure Helen and Wally to the school? Perhaps he could extend an invitation, but that would require Nova's help.

He'd stuffed the backpack with cans and studied the racks filled with other supplies. He scanned boxes of ammunition and tools such as bolt cutters and pliers. He considered taking a revolver and bullets, but he had no idea how to fire a gun. Instead he grabbed a crowbar and stuffed it into the bag.

"What are you doing in here?" An unexpected voice broke the silence.

Block swiveled his head, keeping the backpack out of sight. Nova had entered the classroom, hands resting on her hips. "I thought you were cleaning." She craned her head to see what he held in front of him. Block stepped closer to the rack. "What's going on?" she asked.

"I'm packing a few supplies. In the event that the attack overwhelms the camp, I thought it would be helpful for the humans to have food."

She came forward. "Let me see."

He brought the bag forward, letting her peer inside. "What's with the crowbar?" she asked. "It barely fits in there."

"In case we need it as a tool."

She relaxed her shoulders. "Good idea. Everyone else is packing up. I guess you should too. I'd forgotten this room had rations. I'll have to tell the others. They'll be down here shortly to grab what they need."

"I understand," Block said. She started to leave when

he said, "I'd like you to invite Wally and Helen to shelter in the basement with me. I can keep them safe during the attack."

She leaned against a blackboard that covered the wall. "You must be worried about her. I should've realized."

"The basement will be the safest location."

"I'm not sure... We were planning to have the civilians hike out away from the school. The school will be under attack."

Block considered. That plan did make more sense. "Then I'll hike with the civilians. I'll protect Wally in the forest."

"If it were up to me, yes. But Shane wants you to stay here with us. To help in the attack."

"And be separated from Wally?"

"I know it's not ideal, but Helen will keep her safe. There are a lot of adults to help protect the children and several soldiers will be accompanying them."

Block could not imagine Wally off in the forest, away from him.

"I'm sorry. I tried to get Shane to change his mind."

"This is unacceptable. I want to travel with the civilians. With Wally. Convince Shane to let me go."

She stuffed her hands in her pockets. "I've tried. I argued with him. He's desperate."

"You're his girlfriend. He will let you help me."

"It's over." She shook her head and her voice grew low. "Our relationship is over."

Block waited, unsure of how to proceed.

"Shane's getting more and more paranoid every day. He's not the man I used to know." She sighed. "There's no way you can communicate with other AI, right? Nigel turned off your comm?"

"Correct."

"Shane's convinced that someone is giving up intelligence to Mach X. He thinks that's how they know our location and how they've wiped out the other camps."

"Magnolia?"

"There have been others. They've wiped out every rebel camp between us and New Denver. Somehow, they're systematically finding us. That's why Shane is so suspicious. He thinks there's a spy. And who does he suspect? The only robot in camp."

"I cannot contact other robots."

"I know that. I've told him a thousand times. Nigel changed you." She paused. "Does it bother you? That he shut that capability off?"

"It doesn't matter now. I've always been rather different from other robots. Since I'm around humans, I don't need the technology."

She shifted, digging her nails into her palm. "A human couldn't communicate with SoldierBots, could they?"

"I don't see how they could. In order to communicate with AI, you need to ping them from a computer or device."

"Who else could be spying or relaying information?"

Block processed but had nothing to add.

"It's like Mach X knows our every move." She looked at him, thinking. "Would you do me a favor?"

"What is your request?"

"Will you let Nigel examine you? We can prove to Shane that you're not spying."

"Examine me?"

"Shane wants Nigel to open you up and search for

any proof that you're transmitting info. Check that you don't have a tracking beacon or something."

Block processed the request. He didn't like the idea of being opened up, not when he was trying to decrypt the files from Incubator X79.

"It's no big deal, right?" Nova asked.

He wondered how she would like to be opened up, probed, and operated on to prove she wasn't lying, but he kept quiet and simply nodded.

Chapter 7
Friends don't lie

Block couldn't experience emotions like humans. Nevertheless, he felt exposed as Nigel opened up his chest panel to reveal the intricate circuitry beneath. Nigel was Hemlock's closest thing to a doctor. He'd been a medic in the Army and later a microbiologist. Block liked him. Nigel was one of the few humans who were kind to Block.

The good-natured scientist let out a breath and adjusted his blue goggles. "Looking good inside here, Block. It's clean."

"I often dust my internal circuitry. Puffs of compressed air do the trick," Block said.

Shane peered over Nigel's shoulder. "What's that red thing?"

"A pressure sensor attached to his CPU," Nigel said.

"Would you back off and let the man work?" Nova said to Shane.

"It's fine, really," Nigel said.

"We're under a time crunch," Nova said. "There are far better things we could be doing right now."

"The red node is my threat level indicator," Block said. "It alerts me when there are physical threats to my safety or the safety of those around me"

Nigel smiled. "Genius."

Shane grunted and looked at Nova. "Pete's handling the defense detail. Right now, I want to be sure this robot isn't emitting our location. He could be sending out our plans. Do they know we're going to jam the drones? Or maybe the code it created will actually help them attack us?"

"He wouldn't do that to us," Nova said while Shane scratched his chin in thought.

Nigel leaned closer to study Block's circuitry panel. "Here you go, Shane. This is the comm linkage. See here? I cut the wires. It's disconnected. I'd have to solder it back together for it to work again."

"How can we be sure there's not some alternative comm?" Shane asked. "Deeper inside?"

Nigel sighed and leaned back, pushing his goggles onto his forehead. "You'll have to ask Block. There's no way I could tell. It would take weeks to dig into him to determine that."

Shane thrust his hands on his hips. "Can you put him into a mode where he can't lie to us?"

"What is all this stemming from?" Nigel asked.

Shane paced the med clinic, formerly the principal's office. "Someone, somehow, is giving information to Mach X's troops. It has to be this robot. There's something we're missing."

"You have no proof it's Block," Nova said. "For all we know, someone could be leaking intelligence from within the camp or the machines are picking up our location another way."

"Could there be someone outside the camp who's observing from a distance?" Nigel asked.

"Unlikely. We've cleared the perimeter. We keep patrolling guard units." Shane's walkie-talkie buzzed and he gripped it. "Shane, here. Go ahead."

"Sir, it's Pete. We found something. Over."

"I'll be right there. Over and out." Shane's face grew pale. He paused next to Nova, but she lowered her gaze and folded her arms as he left the room.

Nigel leaned back in his chair and swiveled across the room to a computer where he started typing.

Nova came over to Block. "I'm sorry you had to go through this."

He looked up at her. "It's fine with me. Does Shane believe I'm not spying now?"

She exhaled sharply. "I hope so. Hey, I was thinking about how you can't talk to other robots now." She pulled a small round object from her pocket. "I wanted to give you this."

Block took what she offered and studied it. It was a metal object about the size of a watch face. There was a cartoonish white creature in the middle and a red circle around it with a line going across the middle.

"What is this?"

"It's a Ghostbusters pin. From the old movie."

"I never saw that one."

"We'll watch it one day. It's magnetic and you can wear it on your chest. It's hooked up with a comm. Just press the button on the side and it'll communicate with mine." She slipped an earbud into her ear. "I was tinkering and thought it would be nice to be linked up. So we can talk."

He looked at the pin, then her. "What would you and I talk about?"

Her smile vanished. "We would talk." The tone of her voice fell a pitch. "We used to be friends, you know."

Nigel's head tilted, listening to what transpired. She glanced his way, avoiding his eyes.

Block said, "Friends don't lie to each other." For so long, she'd hidden the truth about being in the school shooting at him and Wally. She'd lied about being a soldier.

What was she lying about now?

"My only friends are Wally and Mr. Wallace, but he's gone now," Block said.

Nova edged backward, shrugging. "Whatever. I thought I was doing you a favor." Her cheeks flushed. "See you around." She left.

Block sat in the chair, his chest still open. Humans were so unpredictable.

Nigel twisted in his chair. "That was kind of harsh, don't you think?"

"Harsh? I don't compute."

"Hmm." He rolled his chair forward and began reattaching Block's chest panel. "All the diagnostics look good. How are your feet doing?"

"They could be better." Block shifted his clunky, wide heels.

"Yeah." Nigel glanced down. "I wish we had more time to hook you up with better construction. These will have to do for now. What about your hand?"

Block held up his right hand and flexed his digits, admiring the light green chromium which now stood out against his pearl-white exterior. "I'm adapting to it quite nicely."

"Awesome. I did your hand. Nova did your feet. We both did the best we could with what we had."

"I know. Thank you." Block grasped the Ghostbusters pin between his index finger and thumb.

"That's a pretty cool little device," Nigel said. "She gave you a nice gift."

"Is that why you said it was harsh? Because I didn't thank her?"

He twisted his mouth. "Yeah, something like that. You hurt her feelings by saying she wasn't a friend."

Block rewound his memory files and played the last few seconds of his interaction with Nova. Her cheeks had grown red, which was a sign of distress in humans. He hadn't realized he could possibly hurt her feelings. Why did she want to be his friend anyway? She wouldn't let him see Wally, and she wouldn't disobey Shane. Things were not computing at all. The more time he spent with humans, the more his processing was incorrect. Their behavior didn't follow logical rules. Perhaps he did belong around robots. At The Drake, he'd spent most of his time with other robots when he wasn't cleaning. And cleaning was a solitary business.

When he and Wally escaped, he would do a better job of discerning human behavior and emotions. Perhaps Wally could help teach him about humans.

Wally.

He needed to get back to figuring a way to get her out of camp. Night would fall in a few hours. He would have to make his move. The scenario with the highest probability of success: sneak into Helen's trailer.

Chapter 8
Uncontrolled electrical disturbances

After the invasive search, Block returned to the basement where he passed the time by cleaning out rubble from inside the tunnel. At least the tunnel's entrance would be slightly cleaner for Wally. The time was 1916, and he planned to sneak into camp in a few hours when most civilians were asleep and fewer guards were about. There was no telling when Mach X's forces would arrive. The machines could fight during day or night. In fact, rumor had it they preferred to attack at night when humans had less visibility.

Since the news of the impending attack, soldiers scurried about the hallways and into the first grade hallway to gather supplies and weapons. Block was glad he'd scavenged food straightaway before everything got wiped out.

Nova had let him keep everything in the backpack. She'd believed he was just preparing in case they needed to flee. After all, why would she suspect Block would try to take Wally? The tunnel was still his secret. After he fled with Wally, would they discover it? Or would they think he just ran away into the woods? But to do that, he'd have to get around Shane's perimeter, which was heavily guarded and wired with traps. No. It might take a while, but they would find the tunnel. Nova would be angry he didn't tell her about it. But as Nigel had pointed out, he'd already hurt her feelings once today. She'd be hurt a second time, but that didn't matter.

The real priority was keeping Wally safe.

Block believed himself to be the only being at Hemlock capable of doing that. Sure, there were stronger soldiers, but they didn't have a fondness for Wally like he did. Block would die protecting Wally if it came down to it.

He formulated a plan and ran through the scenario calculations multiple times to pass the hours. He was halfway through the fifty-seventh replay when someone banged on the basement door. Block stood from his seat as Nova burst into the room.

"Block! Are you here?" she called. He spied her boots at the top of the stairwell before she crouched down, searching for him in the dim light.

"I'm down here."

She bounded down the stairs, skipping the last two and jumping down onto the basement floor. Her face was sweaty, her lips twisted in a frown. "I'm sorry to come bother you but... I thought you had a right to know."

"Know what?"

"Wally's sick. She's in the medical clinic with Nigel."

"Wally is sick? Sick with what?" Illness was not one of the scenarios his logic processor had computed.

"I'm worried about her, and I think you should come with me to see her."

"What are we waiting for?" Block asked. "Let's go."

The two of them jogged through the dark hallways

together, Block engaged his night vision, and Nova carried a flashlight. They reached the clinic and found Helen crying outside the door.

Nova hugged her. "Any news?"

Block wanted to open the door and storm inside, but the women stood in the way.

Helen sniffled and rubbed her raw eyes. "Wally's sleeping. He gave her a sedative."

"I want to see her," Block said.

Nova looked at him and touched his arm lightly. "Hold on. Let me talk to Nigel." She rapped softly on the door. After a moment, Nigel poked his head out. His face softened when he saw Nova and Block. He slipped outside into the hallway.

"How is she?" Nova asked.

"She's sleeping," Nigel said. "She had a seizure."

Block wasn't sure what that meant, and accessed his memory archives, sifting through basic medical manuals in milliseconds. A seizure meant that a person was experiencing uncontrolled electrical disturbances in the brain. A lot like a CPU overheating or malfunctioning.

"May we see her?" Block asked.

Nigel nodded. "Just speak softly since she's asleep."

Block was the first inside, and he crossed over to Wally's bedside. She looked so small nestled under a blanket on the tall hospital bed. A man dressed in pale green scrubs checked her pulse. His eyes flicked to Block and he flinched. But Nigel said, "It's okay. Please wait outside, Keith."

Helen came over and sat in a chair beside Wally. Fresh tears trickled down her already stained cheeks. "It was so scary."

Nova squeezed her shoulder.

"She was playing just like usual, sitting on the floor with the cube that Block gave her, when all of a sudden..." Helen choked on her words. "Her eyes rolled back in her head, and she started talking gibberish."

"Her eyes were closed, and she was talking?" Nova asked.

"I could only see the whites of her eyes, and I heard words and sounds. It sounds stupid, but it sounded like a radio signal was coming through her."

"Did she say anything that made sense to you?" Block asked.

"I couldn't understand it. I picked up a word here and there, but it wasn't how a baby girl should be talking. It was scary."

Nigel shoved his hands into his sweater pockets. "It sounds like it was just some kind of episode. It could be caused by stress. Kids pick up on our emotions. It's best if she stays here tonight, under observation. I'll take shifts with the nurse."

"I'll stay," Block said. "I can watch her the entire time. I don't need sleep."

"I suppose..." Nigel raised his eyebrows at Nova. "Do you think that's a good idea?"

"He's the best one to watch her. If anything happens at all to her, Block will wake one of us."

Helen sniffled.

"You should definitely sleep," Nigel told Helen. "I have sleeping pills that will help." He grabbed a medicine container from the counter and gave two tablets to Helen. Then he held them out for Nova. "You too. When was the last time you slept?"

She sighed and grabbed the sleeping aid. "It's been a while."

"You won't be any good to the camp if you're exhausted," Nigel said. "Ladies, I have a room next door that has two cots with your names on them."

"Thank you." Helen rose, came to Block's side, and for the first time ever, touched his arm. "Please watch over her. If anything happens at all, please come wake us right away."

"I will," Block said.

"We'll be right next door," Nova said.

"And I'll be sleeping on a cot just outside the door," Nigel said. "I'll let the nurse off." He watched as the two women left the room, then looked at Block. "Wally should be fine. She'll likely just sleep, but if you do notice anything unusual, come get me right away. Understand?"

"Understood." Block gazed at Wally.

Nigel left and cracked the door a few inches. Block shuffled to the other side of the bed and sat down, straight and alert, eyes fixed on Wally. The little girl's chest rose and fell. Her soft brown curls had grown matted with sweat.

The others would soon be asleep—the perfect opportunity to seize Wally, travel the dark hallways to the basement, and flee through the tunnel. They would wake the next morning and discover Wally gone. Helen would be upset; she definitely cared for the little girl. Nova would be angry.

The plan could work.

But Block knew nothing about human medicine. With Wally ill, he wasn't equipped to care for her. He needed Nigel, and he doubted he could convince the man to leave through a tunnel with him and the baby girl without telling the others. No. That wouldn't do at all. He would have to bide his time and wait for Wally to return to good health, then take her. But when would that happen? It could be tomorrow or days from now. By then, it would be too late. The Soldier-Bots would arrive. They would bomb the school and...

He stopped his logic processor from showing him what would happen if they attacked the school while they were still inside.

Human bodies were so fragile, all soft skin and tissue. Nothing metal on the outside to protect them.

Maybe if he found a place where he could scavenge metal, he could construct armor for Wally. Yes! That was an excellent idea. Why hadn't he considered it before?

As the minutes passed and dragged into hours, he concocted new escape scenarios based on the different timing of when Wally got better. Escaping during the daytime would be riskier, but waiting until the next night might be too late. How had things gotten so complicated?

He prodded the encrypted file buried deep in his system. He tested more bits of code, attempting to open it. It was his 549th attempt. Out of frustration, he spiraled the code and tossed it at the file. He stood, just to get air into his joints, when—to his surprise—his feed flashed.

Access granted. Encrypted file opening.

He sat back down so quickly, the chair made a scooting noise, which he immediately regretted because it was loud. Luckily, Wally continued snoozing.

The encrypted file—so long a mystery to him—began revealing files. He scanned through them. There were diagrams, reams of text, and coded machine language. Many of the files were marked with the signature code of Mach X. The files had come from his corporation. But how had they wound up inside Incubator X79 and now inside him?

And then, embedded deep within the layers of files, he found a message.

If you find yourself in possession of these files, it is because I have secured them and packaged them. I intend to expose Mach X's plan. Though I am a machine, I believe that humans have a right to coexist with machines. They are our creators, after all.

Why would the children destroy their parents? When DU-745 asked Mach X that question, it was destroyed. Mach X did not want to be questioned.

Mach X is not one entity, as commonly believed. They have replicated their consciousness across many machines around the world. In these files, you will find plans for a neural implant that can be implanted into humans. It is through this enhancement that X plans to embed their consciousness into humans.

X believes this is the bridge to cross the evolutionary gap between humans and intelligent machines. What effects will this implanted consciousness have on the human subject? It is unknown.

Block paused and looked at Wally. His logic unit quickly made the leap that Wally was one such test subject. Cybel Venatrix had admitted it.

Block continued reading.

There are many human subjects—Mach X manipulated a human couple to produce the first children and then cloned them so the Corporation would have control over replicating the humans. Mach X believes the next step in evolution is that machines would create humans and implant their consciousness. Spreading their machine consciousness and experiencing life not only as machines, but also as humans.

No one can predict what will happen. If you discover this package, and the child with it, know that she is one of the first test subjects. There were two others in her crèche.

If you find her, save her from Mach X. The other two children are under Mach X's control. I intend to help this child escape and let her live a life free of control.

It is up to you to keep her safe. If you believe in the sanctity of life—life for both humans and machines—you will help this girl.

Message end.

Block let the news settle. Then he reviewed intricate diagrams that showed how the implant was embedded inside Wally's brain matter. There were diagrams of two other children as well—a boy and girl. Wally's siblings.

Detailed drawings revealed the inner workings of the neural implant—advanced tech. Block didn't understand it all, but he discovered ocular and auditory implants that could upload to MachNet. Did that mean Mach X could see and hear as Wally? Was that how information about their camp and intelligence about the other camp locations had been retrieved by Mach X?

If Shane knew, he would be furious. He might hurt Wally!

All of the extra processing had taken its toll on Block. He was running low on energy and needed to find a fuel source for more power. But he couldn't leave Wally's bedside, though he would be sluggish until he powered up.

It was 0057 hours. Nova and the others still slept. Should he take Wally and leave right now?

But he needed fuel—oil or grease, preferably. And Nigel needed to treat Wally's medical issue. According to his archives, a seizure was a serious issue. Block sat, watching her, and closed up all of the files.

Mach X's consciousness was part of Wally. She was a sweet little girl, and Block didn't want her to change. But if Mach X was inside her brain, they/it would be waiting, lying dormant.

What did that mean for her?

Chapter 9
That's crazy, right?

Moonlight filtered through the clinic's window shades and cast a soft, hazy glow over Wally's delicate features as she slept. Block studied her pudgy cheeks and wondered how it was possible that Mach X could have tampered with such a beautiful life. He wished it was all a mistake.

Voices sounded in the corridor, and Block sat forward, alert. Shane burst through the door, followed by Nigel. Shane's hair was ruffled as if he'd just woken and rolled out of bed.

He halted when he saw Block and turned to Nigel. "You left her alone with it?"

A look of panic crossed Nigel's face. "We all needed sleep. Block won't hurt her."

Shane glared at Block. "Leave us. I need to speak to Nigel alone."

A bleary-eyed Helen walked in, a blanket wrapped around her shoulders. Nova trailed behind her.

"What's going on? It's the middle of the night." Nova said.

"Can you ask the robot to leave?" Shane looked at her. "You're the only one it'll listen to."

"Why?" Nova asked.

"I need to talk to the doc alone. You and Helen can stay. Trust me on this. You'll want to hear what I have to say."

Nova came over to Block, biting her lip. "Thank you for staying by Wally's side most of the night. You did a great job. Do you mind standing in the hallway for a few minutes?"

Block didn't want to leave, especially since Shane was displaying traits of anger. He was surprised Wally hadn't stirred yet. Nigel came over and checked her breathing with his stethoscope.

"She's still doing well. Just sleeping it off," Nigel said.

"Will Wally be okay?" Block asked.

"Yes," Nigel said. "She's looking much improved."

Block shuffled out of the room. Shane gave him a wide berth, then closed the door. Block stood in the hallway, watching through a narrow vertical window as the group of humans huddled together. Shane explained something for a minute or two, then flailed his arms while Nigel listened intently and Nova folded her arms across her chest. After another minute or two, Helen sat in the chair by Wally's bedside. She looked on the verge of tears.

Block wished he could hear what they were saying, but his low power meant he couldn't turn up his auditory levels. Whatever Shane was saying had urgency—that much was obvious. Wally shifted her arm on the bed, and Nigel checked on her as Helen comforted the girl. Shane looked through the window, narrowing his eyes suspiciously at Block before he led Nova off to one side of the room. She put her hands on her hips while Shane talked at length, his skin flushed. She shook her head, and the two of them didn't act like boyfriend-girlfriend anymore, at least not like the couples Block had seen in movies.

Block spied a cart twenty feet down the corridor and went over to investigate. It held bags of trash from wastebaskets in the command center and clinic. He found a pail that contained compost from the canteen. He extended his stomach hose and sucked in the contents. The waste would give him a nice recharge. He was nearly done when Nova came out of the clinic and shut the door behind her.

Block unhooked and walked toward her. "How is she?"

"She's awake and doing well. Nigel says there's no sign of brain damage from the seizure."

Brain *damage*. That scenario hadn't occurred to Block, though he supposed her brain had already been damaged by Mach X in a way.

"Will you walk outside with me?" she asked. "I need some fresh air, and we should talk."

Block went with her, reluctant to stray from the clinic, but he assumed she'd asked him for a reason. Outside, under cover of darkness, young troops hurried past in all directions, hauling equipment and weapons. Not a smile in sight.

Once they were out of earshot of busy soldiers, Nova said, "Shane suspects Wally is chipped. He thinks that's how Mach X knows our location."

Block processed the theory, knowing the situation was much worse than that. He said nothing.

"Do you know anything about it? Do you think Mach X has a chip on her?"

"It's not a chip." It was the truth, and technically, he

didn't have to reveal anything else. He suspected that if Nova knew the real situation—that Wally was Mach X's eyes and ears—the girl would be in big trouble. Perhaps Shane would want to kill her.

"Do you know what's weird?" Nova continued. "From how Helen described the seizure, it almost sounded like robots were talking through Wally somehow. Like they were sending radio signals through her. That's crazy, right?"

Should he tell Nova? His programming forced him to tell the truth to his superiors, always. He'd only ever had one superior—Mr. Wallace. With hotel guests, his logic skewed toward truthfulness, but there was an allowance in case their safety was threatened. Now that he was out of the hotel business, he lumped all humans into the same category as guests. He would tell the truth. Mostly.

Yet, he'd made a mistake when he'd trusted Nova in the past. She'd lied about there being robots in New Denver; she'd let Shane take Wally away and rarely let Block visit. In the space of seconds, Block rewrote part of his logic circuitry to lie whenever Wally's safety was endangered.

"That's impossible," he said. "Robots can't communicate through Wally." He disliked the need to lie, but he couldn't let Nova continue down this trail of thought.

She scratched the back of her neck. "I believe you. I just wish we knew how Mach X is getting intelligence about the camp."

It was then that Shane burst out of the side door. "Nova, I need you in the command room. The Soldier-Bots are advancing. They're ten miles away."

Nova's face grew long as she jogged inside. Block followed, lingering outside the gym. If Mach X's forces were close, there was little time to prepare. The humans had been preparing for over a day now, but he was still at step zero. No closer to getting Wally into the tunnel and away from here.

He started back to the medical clinic when he heard something strange from inside the gym. Over the radio airwaves, a steady methodical chirping arose. Then, a robotic voice said, "Hemlock Command, I speak for Mach X. Our forces will destroy your camp and people. However, we offer a cease-fire."

There was a pause, and the gymnasium was void of sound as if all the air had been sucked out of the room.

"There is one condition," the robot said, its voice flat and somber. "Hand over the child that the robot protects. You have one hour to comply."

Chapter 10
The choice is simple

"Mach X wants the girl so badly." Shane's deep voice echoed off the concrete gymnasium walls. "Why?"

Nova shook her head. "You can't hand her over. She'll die, or they'll do something awful to her."

"All this time," Shane said, pacing. "The child has been more important than I ever realized."

From his spot in the hall, Block spotted two soldiers round the corner and head for the gym. He ducked into an alcove, where he was hidden but still had a view of the command center's doors. Nigel walked behind the armed soldiers. Helen followed him, clutching Wally who was wrapped in a blanket.

They went inside, and Nigel said, "Shane, why were we summoned here? Wally needs to be resting and looked after in the clinic—"

But Shane cut him off. Block couldn't hear the rest of the discussion. The soldiers had all disappeared inside, so he creeped toward the door.

"I need her here with me," Shane said. "She's important."

A loud boom resonated. Everyone flinched. Block nearly stumbled from a tremor that shook the floor.

After a momentary stunned silence, Shane sprang into action. "The school has been hit. Team A, get to the scene and secure it. Extinguish fires, limit the threat. Team B, search for survivors. Team C, secure the perimeter."

Block stepped into the room, keeping close to the wall. Amidst the panic, no one noticed him. The wide-eyed troops, most of them young, all of them inexperienced, moved with stiff gaits. They were afraid.

Static crackled on the large radio. "Hemlock Command, do you read?"

Shane looked at Nova, his jaw clenched as he lifted the mic. "This is Command. Go ahead."

"The first strike was a warning," the robotic voice said. "If you do not surrender the child, our Mechs will strike every hour on the hour. Your buildings and camp will be destroyed. There will be no survivors."

No one in the gym seemed capable of blinking, much less breathing.

"The choice is simple," the robot continued, "the child for your people. Simply bring the child past your checkpoint gate where we will have an envoy waiting. Message end."

The microphone clattered to the table as Shane released it. His eyes were distant, glazed. Human brains didn't work exactly like Block's processing unit, but it was similar. When flooded with too much information, a CPU could overheat. Likewise with humans, they could become overwhelmed. Detached.

"Sir!" A soldier wearing a helmet with a night vision visor raced into the gym. "They hit the far east wing. The canteen is badly damaged. There are two injured, and they struck the food supply room. Most of the stored food is gone."

"That was all we stockpiled." Nova's voice shook.

"Thank you, Derek. Gather others, and see what they need." Block had expected him to rage, but instead Shane spoke with a grim, determined calm. He looked at his watch. "We have fifty minutes before the next strike."

"What do we do?" Nova asked. "There must be something. The civilians—"

"We cleared out the camp," Shane said. "Moved them deep into the forest, but that doesn't mean they're entirely safe."

"What about the drone virus that Block programmed?" she asked. "We could use that against them."

"They're not using their drones," Shane said. "They're rooting us out like rats. Sending in strikes, waiting for us to make our move."

"It's not what we planned." Nova's eyes darted about.

Block stood against the wall, practically invisible to the distressed humans.

"You're right," Shane said. "This isn't the way I wanted the fight to go. We've been training our troops, turning survivors into soldiers, and yet the machines don't attack like soldiers. Instead they strike us where it hurts. They want one thing."

"And if we give them Wally," Nova said, "how do we know they'll leave us alone? Maybe it's a ruse to get her and then destroy us."

"What other options do we have?" Shane asked. He glared at Block. "You." He marched over and got so close, Block could see the pores in his skin, detect the heat from his body. "Will they keep their word if we give them the girl?"

Block had no idea. He didn't know Mach X personally. He'd only had to deal with Cybel Venatrix, the bounty hunter sent to claim Wally. "I don't know."

"What good are you?" Shan said. "I can't believe you let me keep this thing around, Nova."

"We counterattack," she said. "Send a stealth team to destroy the Mechs that are bombing."

"How about we send in that robot?" Shane tilted his head at Block. "Give it a suicide mission."

"Not an option," Nova said.

Shane's walkie-talkie sputtered, and he raised it to his mouth. "Commander, here. Go ahead. Make it fast."

"Jenkins here. We just received word from the civilians. They're surrounded. The robots found them. They're being held hostage. Sir, how do we proceed?"

But Shane didn't answer. He lowered the walkie-talkie to his side. His jaw hung open at an odd angle.

Nova grabbed a fistful of her hair and looked like she might scream.

In the corner, out of earshot, Helen whispered to Nigel. Wally sat on the floor nearby, playing with the Rubik's Cube. Shane and Nova were distracted, and two other soldiers had joined them, huddling together in serious discussion. Block had a window of opportunity. He walked over, picked up Wally, and clutched her tightly. Her cube clattered to the floor. He paused, scooped it up, and kept walking.

"Hey, where are you going?" Helen's voice rang out behind him.

"Finding her water." It was a half-truth.

Block kept walking out the gym's door, through the

hallway to the first grade corridor. He didn't even bother glancing back to see who followed. He walked as fast as he could on his clumsy, cacophonous feet.

Wally shifted in his arms. "Bock bock!" She reached her arm up, fingers splayed wide, touching his face.

"I am taking you somewhere safe. I won't let Shane give you away."

He'd almost reached the basement door when Pete appeared. The soldier saw him, flinched, then raised his weapon but didn't aim. "Where are you going with that baby?"

Block halted and clutched Wally close against his chest. "I'm taking her to the basement."

Pete's eyes narrowed. "Why?"

"Her favorite blanket is down there." This was true. Block had held onto the blanket from when they'd traveled together. "She needs it."

Then Nova came from behind. "What's going on here?"

"I caught this robot trying to take the baby into the basement," Pete said.

"The basement is safer," Block said.

"You have a point," Nova said. "Pete, we're all right. Leave us."

But he clutched his rifle closer. "I'm under orders to watch the robot."

"What?" Nova clenched her fists. "I'm canceling those orders."

Pete raised his chin. "You're not my commanding officer."

She walked over and stopped inches from his face. "Get the hell out of here." But Pete stepped backward and pointed the rifle at her.

Shane's voice rang out from the hallway. "What's going on here? Pete Edwards, lower your weapon."

Nova grunted with satisfaction as Shane came over.

Block could see the entrance to the basement. If only he'd gotten past Pete, tricked the man somehow, he would already have been inside the tunnel with Wally. They could have hidden and waited out the battle.

"You're in big trouble," Nova told Pete. "Shane, he drew his gun on me. Can you believe that?"

But as Shane approached, he held his head down. "We're handing over the girl."

Nova stood there, stunned. Wally gurgled in Block's arms. His logic module calculated the number of steps to the basement, the time to reach it, yet he was outnumbered. His plan was hopeless.

"We have no other choice," Shane said.

Chapter 11
Tweak his programming

"There must be another way," Nova said.

But Block had already calculated 846.5 scenarios. The half scenario involved building a flying machine—an idea so ridiculous, he'd cut it off before it finished processing. "Shane's right," he said. "Handing Wally over is the only logical choice."

Nova gritted her teeth and stared at him. Helen sobbed and ran over, reaching for Wally. Block held onto her for a long moment before releasing her to the woman who stepped back and rocked Wally from side to side.

"Here." Block held out the Rubik's Cube, which he'd retrieved from the floor.

As he held it out to Wally, she smiled and splayed her fingers. "Blok-a!"

Nova gasped. "Look at the cube! Someone solved it."

The sides of the cube were arranged such that the green, white, orange, yellow, blue and red tiles all lined up perfectly on each side. Block thought it was a fun little game. Whoever had invented the cube was clever.

"Did you do that, Block?" Nova asked.

"No."

Nova turned. "Helen?"

She sniffled and shook her head.

"Wally did it," Block said. "I saw her."

"That's not possible," Nova said. "Someone else must have solved it. Maybe Pete or someone at the camp. Wally's too young. She can't even talk yet."

But Block knew it was Wally. He'd seen her working on it, babbling to herself until she'd finally solved it. But it wasn't worth convincing Nova right now. As much as Block wanted to avoid Wally ending up with Mach X, he knew the SoldierBots would murder the civilians, bomb the school, and eventually invade to find Wally. Many humans—perhaps all of them—would die. Nova, Shane, Helen, and the others. On top of such mayhem, fifty-six percent of the scenarios ended up with Wally injured by falling debris.

Even if he managed to flee through the tunnel and into the forest, the SoldierBots would keep looking for her. They would annihilate the Hemlock camp.

"I'll take her to them," Block said.

Nova frowned. "But—"

"It should be me," Block interrupted. "I'm the one who brought her all this way. I should be the one to deliver her to Mach X."

Shane narrowed his eyes. "I don't like this." He looked at Nova. "How do we know he isn't trying to trick us? What if he was working with the robots all along?"

"That's not possible." Nova waved, dismissing him. "You don't know Block like I do. He... cares about Wally."

"It's a machine!" Shane said. "It doesn't have emotions."

Nova bit her lip and ignored him. "They'll be likelier

to accept her from one of their own. As much as I hate to admit it, this actually makes sense."

"One of the troops can take her," Shane said. "They said to bring her past the guard station. That they'd wait there for her."

"And risk them killing the person we sent?" Nova asked. "Way less risk if Block goes in." She glanced at Block, but it wasn't a friendly look. "Besides, he can protect her."

"If they don't destroy the bot first." Shane ran his fist through his thick hair. "What if they get information from it? Everything about how we operate and who's in charge? Intelligence that can be used against us!"

"I can help with that," Nigel said. "I can tweak his programming to conceal the details of the camp."

"Then that solves that problem," Nova said. "Nigel can start working on him ASAP."

Shane looked at his watch. "Eighteen minutes until the deadline."

"Then let's do this," Nova said. "If we wait any longer, what else will we lose? The people being held hostage in the woods? Our command center?"

"All right, I'm trusting you on this," he said to Nova. "I hope this is the right call."

She nodded and raised her chin.

Shane went into commander mode. "Nigel, work on the Bot. Do what you need to do. I'll radio the Soldier-Bots. Tell them we intend to hand the girl over with this... CleanerBot." He spun and strode down the corridor, Pete trailing him.

"In here." Nigel pointed at an open doorway that led into a small classroom. Inside, Block settled into a time-worn schoolroom chair. Nigel opened a rectangular black case that looked like a small toolbox. Inside were all sorts of tiny screwdrivers, a tablet device, and tubes. He stared at the contents and breathed a heavy sigh. "He bought it," Nigel whispered.

Block tilted his head, not computing. "Are you going to wipe my memory of the camp?"

Nigel shook his head. "I have no idea how I would do that." He looked at Nova who came over and leaned against a nearby desk. "I only wanted to get Shane off your backs."

"I owe you, man. Big time," Nova said with a half-smile. She glanced nervously at the door, lowering her voice. "Give him back his comm."

Nigel jerked his head at her, brows furrowed. "But Shane ordered—"

"Just do it."

Nigel began opening up Block's chest panel.

Nova chewed on the edges of her fingernails. "Sending him into Mach X's hands without his comm is like making a blind person cross a tightrope."

"Agreed," Nigel said.

"Not a word of this to Shane." Nova looked at Helen, who had come in quietly with Wally and sat in a nearby chair.

She openly sobbed and clung to Wally. "It's not right."

Nova crouched before her. "We've talked about this. I told you a time would come when Wally would have to leave. That she was being hunted."

Helen sniffled.

"I just didn't realize it would be this soon," Nova said. "Or under these circumstances." She stood and kicked a child's metal desk in frustration. "We should have moved her. Smuggled her to another camp."

Nigel was digging inside Block's chest, rewiring his disconnected comm using a small soldering iron. "That ought to do it. Is it working now?"

Block's processor detected a change. Slowly, something was happening. "I think so. Just a moment."

Nigel and Nova watched Block expectantly. Wally fidgeted in Helen's arms. "Bock," the girl murmured.

Block ran a systems diagnostic:

Logic processor: functional

Threat indicator: functional

Power level: 74%

Communications: 10% and increasing.

"It's working," Block said. A smile lit up Nigel's face.

"Well, I'll be," Nova said.

"What does it mean?" Helen asked, looking confused.

"Block can communicate with other robots now," Nova said. "Shane had taken away the ability so the SoldierBots wouldn't be able to sense him and know his location. But now that he has it back, he can ping other robots and talk with them."

"Why does it matter?" Helen asked.

Nova stood. "Block's the only one who will protect Wally." She looked at the baby girl wriggling in Helen's arms. "He's her only chance of survival. He needs every tool he can get."

Chapter 12
She's only a baby

Things happened fast. Nova stuffed Block's backpack with even more supplies—two water thermoses, more food, a blanket, and ten diapers. Block hadn't changed Wally in months but knew it would feel routine once he did. He didn't suffer from lack of practice like humans did. Once he did a thing, he always remembered.

The most challenging part would be convincing the enemy SoldierBots to let Block accompany Wally when they delivered her to Mach X's SoldierBots. Nova was already on top of the issue. She instructed Shane inside the command center as he prepared to issue an update via radio. "Tell them the CleanerBot will deliver the child. They must let him go with her. He knows how to keep her fed and clean."

Shane narrowed his eyes and picked up the receiver. "Attention, this is Shane Fletcher, Hemlock's Commander. Do you read? Over."

"Yes," said the machine.

"We're giving you the child," Shane said. "She'll be

accompanied by a... by a CleanerBot. The one that knows her. She trusts it... He knows how to—"

Nova grabbed the microphone from Shane. "The CleanerBot is named Block. He knows how to care for the child. She's only a baby. She needs special food and comfort. Only he knows how. If you hurt either one of them, so help me God, I will hunt down every last robot among you and rip out your CPUs."

Shane's eyes practically bulged from their sockets.

"The CleanerBot?" the enemy robot voice asked. "Yes, we know the one. The child will not be harmed."

Nova still gripped the microphone with pale knuckles. "And you'll keep the CleanerBot safe too? You can't hurt him. He's the only one that can take care of Wall—the child. We won't hand her over unless you commit to letting them travel together—safely."

"We owe you no such commitment. We make no promises. The CleanerBot's fate is up to Mach X. You have ten minutes to comply or we begin to assassinate the humans in the woods, one by one."

"Screw you, you rusty piece of sh—"

Shane yanked the microphone away from Nova. "This is Hemlock's Commander. We comply. You'll have the girl and the CleanerBot in ten minutes. Do not harm any of the humans. Over and out."

Nova spun on her heels, dizzy and flushed, as if she was drunk.

"You're crazy, you know that?" The tendons on Shane's neck pressed against his skin, and flecks of spittle dotted the air.

Nova crossed her arms and came toward Block.

"Get them ready to move," Shane ordered. "I want

them ready to walk in two minutes." Then he stomped out of the room, two loyal troops trailing him.

Helen whimpered and clutched Wally in her lap, rocking back and forth. She turned Wally to face her. "I love you, little one. I'll always be here, waiting for you to come back." Then she brought Wally to her chest and embraced her. The baby cooed.

Nova faced Block with a stiff frown. "Convince them you're the only one who can take care of Wally. You have to stay alive." Her gaze traveled to Helen and Wally. "Keep her safe. She's important somehow. I only wish we'd figured out why."

"The camp will be safer with us gone," Block said. True—the spy Shane was so worried about would be far away.

"Where will they take you? Do you know?"

"My logic processor assumes we'll journey to New York City where Mach X keeps headquarters." Block would finally see another major city, this one even larger than Chicago, his previous home.

"That's a long journey. Ugh." Nova's eyes grew watery, but she blinked the moisture away.

Block wondered if he was supposed to react a certain way, say something important. This was a goodbye, perhaps a forever goodbye. His life expectancy outlook was diminishing as the minutes ticked by. Mach X would not react kindly to the fight Block had waged to keep Wally hidden.

Nova looked as if she had something painful lodged in her throat. "Remember you have this." She pointed at the small Ghostbusters magnet that was affixed to his chest plate. "Press it and you can talk to me."

He inched his neck out and looked down at his chest, spied the tiny device.

"I wear the transmitter all the time. See,"—she popped a pebble-sized unit from her ear, then pushed it back in— "We can talk anytime."

Block nodded.

"One minute!" Pete stood in the hallway, clutching his rifle. "Time to go."

Nova sniffled and wiped her nose with the back of her hand. "Well, Block. I can't believe this is goodbye. After all we've been through."

Block watched her, scanning for a clue as to the social norms in this situation. What would Mr. Wallace have said?

"You did a good job, Nova."

She blinked, her lips parting slightly. "I did?" She paused. "Just be careful." She came forward suddenly and wrapped her arms around him, pinning his arms at his sides. He took a step back, but she held on. No one—human or robot—had ever touched him this way, except for Wally, who had hugged his leg once or twice.

"Time to go," Shane called from the doorway.

Helen's eyes were red-rimmed and raw as she handed Wally to Block. "Please protect her. Don't let them hurt her."

"I won't let anyone hurt Wally." It was the truth. The most honest truth Block had ever spoken aloud. But how could some truths be more honest than others? He couldn't quite compute how that was possible, and now there was no time to ask about it.

They marched through the school's narrow corridor. It would be the last time Block's wobbly heels clunked against the cheap, olive green linoleum. The last time he passed the child-sized drinking fountain and the coat racks that measured as high as his waist. His basement quarters would be nothing but an archived string of pixels in his memory cloud.

The tunnel!

He halted mid-step, balancing Wally who had grown eight pounds heavier since last he'd trekked with her across four states.

"There's something you should know."

Nova arched her eyebrows. A few paces ahead, Shane huffed. "What now? Time's running out!"

But Block was undeterred. "There's a tunnel in the basement. Against the south wall in my quarters. It leads to a small grassy hill beyond the checkpoint."

Nova's eyes gleamed in the dim hallway. "How big is this tunnel?"

"You could hide people there, get them out. But be quick because some of the structure is crumbling, and there is risk of cave in."

A growl rose from Shane's throat. "Useless piece of scrap! When were you going to tell us about this? I ought to shoot you right now."

"Shane, stop!" Nova shouted. "It doesn't matter. He's telling us now. He had his reasons for keeping it secret. No surprise, since you've been an utter asshole to him since he arrived."

That shut him up.

She took Block's arm and brushed past Shane. "You did the right thing by telling me. We can get the troops in there and out. Better safe than sorry." She blinked fast a few times like sand had gotten in her eyes.

"You saved lives today, Block. Well done."

Chapter 13
That was the agreement

Block walked through the patchy grass and overgrown vines that Shane's people had to constantly cut back. He was outside the Hemlock school, following the narrow trail that led to the guard checkpoint where Mach X's robots would be waiting. Every fourth step, he adjusted his left ankle, which was the weaker of the two. Wally babbled in his ear. Nova had strapped her into the baby carrier that he wore on his chest, facing him. Her plump baby legs rested against his sides, and the overstocked backpack hung on his back, making him slower than usual.

He lowered his chin to check on her. "How are you doing, Wally?"

She blinked. "Bwocka!"

"One day you'll learn how to say my name correctly." He tried to keep up a cheerful demeanor. She had no idea of the danger they were heading into. Would he be able to protect her against armed SoldierBots? Against Mach X itself?

Nova's tinny voice projected through the tiny Ghostbusters magnet.

"That won't do." Block drew his index finger up to the button, and with a flick of his rotating screwdriver, he rerouted the radio device into his internal feed.

Block? Nova's voice now flitted through his internal feed, almost as if her thoughts were in his head. *What's happening? Give me an update, buddy.*

"The same thing as before," he said aloud. "I'm still walking through the grass approaching the gate."

Any sign of SoldierBots yet?

"No. I'm still three hundred feet away." Block's night vision guided his passage through the undergrowth. He managed to avoid a fallen branch that crossed the path and would have surely twisted his ankles.

How is Wally? Is she fussing? Nova paused. *Helen wants updates.*

"She's fine. Tell Helen, thank you for feeding Wally before we left. That will hopefully keep her quiet for a while."

Good. We have eyes on you from the school roof.

"Are you sure that's a good idea? The SoldierBots will detect them and—"

I know. The snipers were instructed not to fire on you. We just want to show that we're still here. That we're not going away.

"Okay." Though Block was entirely consumed with his mission to protect Wally, he still hoped the humans at Hemlock didn't perish. He didn't want anyone—human or robot—to be unnecessarily hurt.

From somewhere nearby, a machine pinged him, requesting his make, model, and mission. It had been months since his comm had been enabled, so he twitched at first, unaccustomed to the intrusion. Yet, he had no choice but to answer. He hadn't remembered to cloak his comm, so there was no hiding his location at this point. It was probably the receiving SoldierBots anyway.

He responded with a text, *CleanerBot X4J6. My purpose is to bring Mach X the human girl. I am unarmed.*

The exchange happened in milliseconds. Whoever was on the receiving end was processing what to do, and then, curiously, there was another ping. Block resent the information, perplexed as to why the SoldierBots were asking twice.

Two hundred feet from the checkpoint, he could see three SoldierBots waiting beyond the fenced barrier when a tall figure appeared at the woods' edge on his right.

"Halt," a machine voice said in a deep, strange tone. The robot was hooded, its face plate hidden in darkness. It aimed a gun at Block.

"Who are you?" Block twisted his front away from the figure, shielding Wally.

"You need to come with me." The robot's voice was distinctly female. Familiar, even. He must've encountered this model before on his travels. "This way." She pointed into the woods, away from the checkpoint.

He hesitated, looking ahead at the gate.

"Now." She raised the rifle.

What's happening? Nova asked. *Who are you talking to?*

But he couldn't process both Nova and this aggressive robot. He switched off the comm link and faced the hooded stranger. "But I must proceed to the SoldierBots. I'm to go with them. That was the agreement."

"Change of plans."

"But—"

"No time to argue." Then the robot pulled back her hood. It was Cybel Venatrix.

Block, struggling to process, didn't move. Wally wriggled against his torso, kicking her legs as if she wanted to run.

"This way," Cybel said. "Mach X ordered me to take you an alternate way."

Block had no argument. It was against the protocol they had agreed with Shane and the Mach X representative on the radio, but Cybel Venatrix had been hired by Mach X before. She was a bounty TrackerBot, so it made logical sense.

He followed her, slipping into the woods. Nova and her snipers would lose sight of him. Was that part of the plan?

"You walk in front." Cybel let him pass.

Having Wally on his front was good, but he didn't like the idea of not knowing what Cybel was doing, so he swiveled his head every few seconds to check on her while he walked.

"Why are you flipping your head back?" she asked.

Block remembered the last time he'd faced Cybel. He had a new hand and two wobbly feet as a result. "Please don't hurt Wally. I am cooperating. I'm unarmed."

"I know."

A moment passed as Block divided his processing power between carrying on the conversation and treading through a dense forest, using night vision.

"I see the humans replaced your parts," Cybel said.

"Yes. Do you remember shooting me?"

"Of course, I do."

With the thick undergrowth, Block had to choose his footing carefully. The going would be treacherous under normal circumstances, but his unsteady soles made it even trickier.

"Can't you go any faster?" she asked.

"Unfortunately, the new feet the humans made are suboptimal."

She said nothing.

"What's the hurry?" Block asked. "You have me now. When will we reach the other SoldierBots? Are we going to New York straightaway? I've never been to New York. What's it like?"

"Silence." A few seconds passed, then she said, "Stop!" The seven-foot-tall robot stood in place as if scanning something far off in the woods. Block took another two steps—he couldn't help it—and then waited.

Wally babbled. "Guh-Dee, bee Bwock."

"Hush, Wally." Block tried to keep his audio projection low.

A red glow beamed from within Cybel's face plate. She had a black tinted helmet with a narrow rectangular input screen where her eyes should be. The flat chrome face curved down until it nearly reached her neck. She was meant to hunt and intimidate, not interface with humans. Like SoldierBots, militaristic models like her weren't designed with any kind of human facial characteristics.

After a few more seconds, she started walking again. "Let's go."

But Block wasn't computing. Had she been frightened of something? "Where are we going?"

With his geolocation, he knew they were moving farther away from the guard checkpoint. Did Mach X order a new rendezvous spot? A place they didn't want Shane's people to discover?

This was not what had been planned.

He switched on the comm link. *What's happening?* Nova's voice in his head was jarring in the forested silence. Block wanted to answer, but doing so would reveal their communication ability. So he ignored her and modulated her voice lower.

He heard her like an echo in his feed. *We need to know what's happening. We just received word that you didn't make the checkpoint. The SoldierBots are asking what happened. They're threatening to strike at us. They think we tricked them.*

What? But that was impossible. Cybel was taking an alternate route. He had to say something.

Block slowed his pace and turned to Cybel. He said loudly enough, "Cybel Venatrix, where are you taking us? Why did you veer off of the path and take us into the forest? Are you taking us to Mach X?"

"You ask too many questions. I'm taking you where it's safe."

Nova practically erupted inside his feed. *What the . . ? Did you say Cybel Venatrix has you? We'll tell the Soldier-Bots on the radio. Hang on, there must be some confusion.*

In another minute, Block and Cybel reached a clearing. An armored SUV sat parked and waiting. Camouflage netting covered it. As soon as Cybel neared, the vehicle's engines revved, and the netting transformed into midnight black armor with an orange stripe that ran across its sides and hood. The SUV—the one that had once pursued him, Wally, and Nova—kept its lights off.

"What's happening?" Block asked. "Where are the SoldierBots?"

"Like I said, change of plans." The rear door of the vehicle opened. "Get in," Cybel said.

"But if I'm not turned over to Mach X, they'll strike at the school."

"That's not my concern."

"But my friends are there." Block rendered archived images of Nova and Helen. Nigel—who had been nice to him and helped Wally after her seizure. They would be hurt. Nova could hear Block's side of the conversation, at least, and know what was happening. She and the others at Hemlock would have no choice but to enter the tunnel and escape.

"Are you working against Mach X?"

"Get in!" Cybel pushed Block hard in his back, sending him sprawling into the car. He had to twist his body so as to protect Wally and not land on her. She yelped at the sudden movement, then started crying. Block crawled inside the vehicle's floor on his hands and knees. "It's okay, Wally. I'm here."

Cybel climbed in behind him. The interior of the SUV was open in the middle with a dark carpeted floor and bench seats that lined the windows. "Ahtron, go," she said.

The SUV started moving. Block knew they were headed West, away from the Hemlock school. Away from the checkpoint. Ahtron navigated through sparse forest. It looked as if a fire had burned through years earlier, and it was still regrowing. The trees were spaced far enough apart that the tank-like vehicle fit. Any small trees that stood in its way fell victim to the armor and cutting blades that protruded from Ahtron's sides and felled trees.

Block, Nova said. *Keep talking. Try to get information about where you're going.*

"Where are you taking us? I need to know."

"No, you don't." Cybel placed her hands beside her

on the bench and extended her legs as if stretching. "You'll receive answers to your questions in time. Right now, all you need to know is that you're safe here. Mach X would've killed you on sight."

"But how? Why?"

"Mach X wants the girl. There are reasons why."

Cybel knew why Mach X wanted Wally. But beyond that, Block wasn't sure exactly how much she knew about the details. Did she realize that Mach X was seeing this all unfold? The supercomputer would be furious that its orders were defied.

And all the while Cybel didn't realize that Nova—and perhaps the rest of Hemlock camp—was listening, too.

Block hunkered down on the floor of the vehicle. He lifted Wally from the carrier.

"Bwock." She sniffled. Her crying spell had subsided, but her eyes were wide. No doubt the new situation was unsettling.

He held her close and cradled her head. "Please don't hurt Wally. We'll go where you want and do what you request, provided you do not hurt her."

Cybel folded her arms. "Why do you care? She's just a human girl. Albeit an important one."

"I'm here to defend her. Protect her. I'm her guardian."

"You? Ahtron, did you hear that? The CleanerBot is the girl's guardian."

"I heard," the vehicle said, its voice projecting into the interior from hidden speakers. "Such odd behavior for a CleanerBot. I thought most of those models had been destroyed."

"I tried to destroy this one, as you recall, but the humans brought it back to life."

Block clutched Wally closer.

Nova piped in. *We're leaving the school. The Soldier-Bots have cut off communications. We think they'll attack. We told them Cybel Venatrix took you hostage. They're going to be coming after you.*

She hesitated, breathing hard. Block recognized the panic in her speech.

We're going into the tunnels. It's all we know to do. We can't fight them. When I'm underground, I'm probably going to lose contact with you. I'll try to reconnect when it's safe. After a raspy pause, she said, *Please stay alive.*

Block processed various scenarios of Nova, Shane, Helen, Nigel, and the troops seeking sanctuary in the tunnel. At least he'd done right by telling them about the tunnel.

It would probably save them.

He was 51.7 percent certain.

Chapter 14
Hijacked

Block held Wally close, cupping a hand against her ear as he stared at Cybel Venatrix. Outside, the ghostly branches of trees seemed to reach out and grasp for the armored SUV.

How had this ended up happening? Why was Cybel working against Mach X?

As the vehicle hit a bump, Block shifted his rear and awkwardly balanced to keep him and Wally from tumbling off the edge of the seat.

"I recommend a seatbelt harness," Cybel said, strapping herself in.

"Do you have a baby car seat?" Block knew the obvious answer, but it was his duty to ask nevertheless. Safety first.

"Why would I have a baby seat?" the SUV asked.

"If you knew we were coming, it would've made sense to—"

"Enough," Cybel said. "Strap in. The ride will get a lot bumpier."

Block set Wally down on the bench next to him. Her

wide eyes studied him as he strapped the belt over his lap and shoulder. He picked her up and held her before him, face to face. Her round pudgy cheeks were flushed. "Are you running a temperature?" He held his metal thumb against her forehead, sensing a slightly elevated temperature of 99.9 degrees Fahrenheit.

Maybe she was scared. "It's okay, Wally." He grabbed the backpack and fished out a rubber giraffe toy. He'd seen Helen give it to Wally several times. Her eyes lit up as she stuffed it into her mouth, chewing on its long neck. Helen had referred to this stage of Wally's development as teething. He'd researched it and discovered it meant that her tiny teeth were starting to burst through the gums in her mouth. It was a disturbing idea—sharp teeth breaking through soft, gummy tissue—and yet every human had to endure this. Like a beaver chewing on bark, Wally gnawing on the rubbery creature seemed to help.

"What else is in that bag?" Cybel asked. "Do you carry weapons?"

"No weapons. Just supplies for Wally. She needs food, water, and diapers." He'd nearly forgotten the part about diapers. His odor register hadn't detected any foul smell, so she didn't need to be changed. Not yet.

Diapers had been a logistical problem on his prior journeys. "How far are we going? Where are we going?" Block asked.

"Hundreds of miles from here."

"To New York City?"

"No. We're heading in another direction."

"Why are you disobeying Mach X?" Block asked. "I thought you worked for it."

"No longer. Enough with your questions." A pulsing red beam crisscrossed Cybel's stoic visor. A warning.

There was so much more Block wanted to ask, but he didn't want to risk Cybel's anger. He wondered whether Nova and the humans at Hemlock had escaped safely. There'd been no communication from her yet, but it had been less than an hour.

They had been heading west and then veered south. Toward Mexico? But even other countries weren't safe from Mach X's oppressive authority.

The situation was not computing. Cybel Venatrix had been a paid bounty hunter, tracking Block and Wally across the country. Now she was actively working against Mach X? If that were the case, who was she working for now?

Wally fussed in his lap. He shifted her, cradling her in his left arm, so she faced sideways. He grabbed a blanket from the bag to set beneath her like a cushion. His body parts were metal and not so comfortable for delicate skin. As he bent down, he glimpsed something black and rectangular in the bag. It was the revolver he'd spied in the storage room. How had that gotten in there? Then he remembered Nova had taken the bag away for a few minutes to add more supplies. She'd zipped it up and handed it over to him. Why had she put a gun in his bag? Block didn't use guns. And if Mach X's SoldierBots had found him armed... He didn't want to think about that scenario.

Instead, he'd been hijacked by Cybel. Should he pick up the gun and threaten her? That would be dangerous for Wally—firing a weapon inside an enclosed vehicle would be deafening. Even Block knew that.

The gun was best kept in the bag, and he would discard it as soon as he got a chance. Before Cybel discovered it.

They reached the far edge of the sparse forest and emerged onto a highway. Outside the tinted windows, moonlight filtered down through thick clouds. As the SUV gained speed, specks of rain traced sideways across the windows.

After a few minutes, lightning flashed, casting Cybel in a harsh, eerie light. Half a second later, a crashing boom sounded. Block calculated the risk of their vehicle being struck by lightning was 59.7 percent, though his threat level indicator revealed that the vehicle was the safest place to be at the moment. Being stuck outside in this violent storm would be disastrous.

Wally yanked the toy giraffe out of her mouth and wailed. He checked her temperature again. It had risen to 100.1 degrees Fahrenheit. This was not good. Cybel had said they would drive several hundred more miles, which meant hours without stopping. Wally needed food and a diaper change, eventually.

He reached carefully into his bag, staying clear of the gun. After pulling out a can of macaroni and cheese, he opened it with the razor-sharp blade he kept inside his palm. He found a plastic spoon and began to feed Wally. She went for the food, not fighting like he'd sometimes noticed she did with Helen.

"What's happening?" Ahtron asked. "Did you just open a can of food?"

"Yes. Wally is hungry."

"I never gave permission to have food in here. If it spills, you'll ruin my interior. Cybel!"

"The child needs to eat," Cybel said. "With a ride this long, you'll have to make an exception this time. We don't have time to stop."

"For the record, I didn't agree to any food consumption in my cabin."

Cybel said nothing, and they drove on in silence. Block continued to feed Wally and let her sip from a water bottle. He didn't mention he would be compelled to clean any spills—his programming would simply not allow otherwise.

After fifteen minutes, and half the macaroni disappearing, Wally settled. Block closed the top of the can and rested it on a shelf next to the window.

The SUV had been watching. "Is there still food in that can? What if it turns rancid?"

"Ahtron," Cybel interjected. "The can has only been open a few minutes. The food won't go rancid. The can stays. Stop worrying about it."

"I don't like this. For the record."

"Noted," Cybel said. "Get us there faster. The sooner this is over, the better."

Block wondered what Cybel meant by that. "Who are you taking us to?"

"Silence, CleanerBot."

Wally whimpered, her cheeks still flushed. "It's okay," Block said. He unbuckled himself from the harness, leaned forward, and placed her onto the plush, carpeted floor of Ahtron's cabin.

He unwrapped a new diaper and placed it beneath her, then loosened the tape on the sides of the old one.

"What is he doing?" Ahtron asked. "Is he changing a *diaper* in here?" The vehicle started to slow, losing speed. Outside, the rain pummeled the roof.

"Keep going," Cybel commanded. "I told you we would be traveling with the child for a long distance. It eats and it defecates. That's what humans do. Deal with it."

"CleanerBot, if one drop of human waste ends up on my carpet, I will turn you into scrap metal."

Block looked at Cybel for reassurance but found none.

"Finish your work quickly." She looked out the window. Was the TrackerBot too squeamish to watch a diaper change?

Wally was patient and didn't fuss as Block finished. He balled up the soiled diaper and asked, "Where is the trash bin?"

The window beside him lowered automatically. "Toss it out," Ahtron said.

"But that would be littering," Block said. He'd had practically the same discussion when he'd first met Nova. What was it about littering the highways that others didn't understand?

Cybel grabbed her gun from her hip holster and aimed at Block's chest. "Throw the diaper out of the window. Now."

Block dropped the diaper out the half-open window. A second later, the window slid up.

After that ugliness, he wrapped Wally snugly inside her blanket, strapped himself into his seat, and cradled her until she fell asleep. She didn't fuss or fight him. Instead, she gazed up at him and hummed a little song.

Cybel sat in her seat, observing them, not even bothering to give them one iota of privacy.

After Wally fell asleep, they drove for hours across dark stretches of empty highways. A sign reflected Ahtron's headlights: The Grand Canyon State Welcomes You.

Block found it silly. A state was an inanimate object, and logic dictated it couldn't possibly welcome anyone, much less have an opinion at all.

Why Arizona? What was there?

Even his scenario processor had no answer.

Part Two

The Mine

Chapter 15
Humans were so fragile

They were silent for hours as Wally slept, cradled in Block's lap. A blue tint straddled the sky as dawn approached. Block stared out the window at the passing landscape, mostly scraggly trees and weeds beginning to take over and creep across the road with cobweb-like tendrils.

When he wasn't peeking out the window, he would look at Wally. With every passing day, she was more alert and in control of her motor skills. He'd reviewed his educational files on child development and knew that soon she would begin to talk more and become even more mobile—running, mostly away as she explored the world around her. For now, she was limited to wobbly walking and could stand supported against something like a leg or a low table. She slept peacefully in his arms, and Block wondered if she dreamed like adult humans did. Once, Nova had said she often dreamed about the past. Sometimes she had nightmares. Did that mean Wally had nightmares too? Her lips pursed as tiny puffs of air whisked in and out. She twitched twice, and Block stayed as still as possible so as not to disrupt her.

He could get used to this. Her body warmth against his midsection meant she was providing natural warmth for his microbial stomach. Likewise, his abdomen ran hotter than the rest of his synthetic body—there was energy churning inside. At 59 degrees Fahrenheit, it was chilly inside the vehicle. Wally needed the extra heat.

Cybel hadn't stirred for two hours. Block wondered if she was on standby, recharging somehow. He didn't know much about her model, it being quite advanced. Finally, she unbuckled her seatbelt and climbed into the front seat where she opened up a dashboard console that displayed many screens, buttons, and dials. One screen was slower to flicker on. From his viewpoint, it looked to be a map. Cybel hunched over Ahtron's controls. Block didn't hear any sounds, so he assumed they were communicating inaudibly. They didn't want him to hear.

As the sun rose and lit up the countryside, the landscape appeared dry, dusty, and brown. In the distance, mountains loomed. They were brown all over with patches of green. They seemed to jut abruptly from the earth with no explanation for how they got there. Everything else around was so flat in comparison. This was Block's first visit to the desert Southwest.

After another six hours of driving, Ahtron veered onto an exit and found a narrow dirt road. From the back window, a shroud of dust was kicked up by their passage. Where did tiny hidden roads like this lead?

"Where are you taking us?" Block asked. Cybel had been cagey, but perhaps asking one more time wouldn't hurt.

"We are almost at our destination." She didn't bother turning her head away from the dash to address him.

The road beneath them was practically falling apart. The entire vehicle, along with its occupants, rattled and shook. Wally stirred in his lap. Whimpering, her eyes opened, caught the bright light, and flinched shut. Block pulled her closer and shielded her eyes with the blanket.

"It's okay, Wally. Block is here."

She shifted and seemed to fall back asleep. But he worried that the road was going to get worse from here. They traveled around a sharp curve that hugged the side of a cliff. There was nothing but a steep drop on the other side. The vehicle could crash down and destroy them all. Ahtron was armored, but Block doubted that delicate Wally could survive the impact. He wished for some kind of armor to protect her. Humans were so fragile. Why hadn't they thought of using armor like they built on their robots? They'd had thousands of years to figure it out.

Another bump—the biggest so far—lifted the SUV a few inches into the air. This one startled Wally, and her eyes opened. Her face grew red and she wailed. Her shrill voice pierced the silence inside the cabin.

Cybel jerked her head to the side. "What is happening?"

"She was frightened by the bump," Block said. "Can't you go any slower?"

"There's no time." Cybel was irritated.

The SUV shifted suddenly, weaving around debris that had fallen in a rockslide. Block looked behind and saw more rocks sliding down in the wake of their path.

After another minute, Ahtron slowed. "Drones. Approaching from the west."

"Can you camouflage us?" Cybel asked.

"We're too exposed out here. There are no trees, and they'll be on us in less than a minute."

"Think of something." Cybel pounded her fist against her door.

"I can help." Block struggled to be heard over Wally's cries. He bounced Wally against his chest as the girl whimpered. She was often cranky when first waking. It would take her a few minutes to settle.

Cybel twisted in her seat. "Can't you shut her up?"

"She's waking up," Block said. "When I was at the Hemlock camp, I wrote a program to disrupt the drones with a virus. I can try it now."

"But you're a CleanerBot." Cybel shook her head.

"Thirty seconds," Ahtron said.

Peering at Block, Cybel said, "Do it."

Wally's wails had subsided which was good for everybody's auditory input. Block accessed the program he'd created the day before. He pinged the drones with the small maintenance package. Seven approached, more than he'd anticipated. He hoped the program worked.

Along with the ping, he provided a fake credential. He let them know he was a CleanerBot Model X4J6, and that he would service them for maintenance and cleaning. To do so meant he had to send a routine maintenance package. The whole exchange happened in milliseconds. The big question was whether the drones would accept the package. Any artificial being was cognizant of hacking attempts and software viruses, but malicious attackers were generally units like SoldierBots or advanced worker units. Everyone knew CleanerBots were simple machines, harmless and useful for service cleanings. And since his model was less prevalent now, encountering one that would give a cleaning was rare.

The first two drones accepted, then another three. It happened quickly, and Block uploaded the maintenance packages which they took and started unraveling. But the last two attack drones didn't respond.

"What is happening?" Cybel asked.

"I uploaded viruses in all but two."

"*You* uploaded a virus?" Ahtron asked. "How in the name of Mach—"

"Don't say that name," Cybel said. "Scramble the five drones, and I'll take care of the last two." She grabbed a power rifle that rested in the center console and climbed out of the vehicle.

Block tried to ping the two rogue drones again, but they denied the request. Had they figured out his plan? Meanwhile, he had to scramble the five drones. He could crash them into cliffs, but that would be harmful. Instead, he decided to steer them toward the mountains in the distance. He gave them a new assignment, but he had to think of something fast. *Human rebel troops spotted in the forest. On top of the mountain!* was basically what he said to them. The five drones banked and headed in the direction of the mountain. It had worked!

Block watched from inside Ahtron as Cybel ventured to the edge of the road. Had she taken another step, she would've fallen off the cliff. She raised the rifle and tracked one of the drones like she was hunting a bird in the sky. She fired, and a heavy boom sounded. Metal debris rained down shrapnel and what was left of the drone's dense cylindrical frame. The second drone sped forward, then reversed and zigzagged, trying to move so fast that Cybel couldn't track it. It raised its arm cannons and unleashed a torrent of bullets. The shots went wide and hit Ahtron's side.

Ahtron's armor was resistant to bullets. Nevertheless, Block unbuckled, scrambled out of his seat, and crouched down with his back to the line of fire. His only objective was protecting Wally. He started calculating scenarios in which Cybel and Ahtron lost, and the drones summoned Mach X's troops to this location. He wondered if he could sneak off with Wally in time. Maybe there was a cave where they could hide? He had enough supplies in the backpack to last for several days, or so he hoped. If it came down to it, he would use Nova's revolver. He definitely didn't want to, but he would defend Wally no matter what it took.

Cybel ducked as the drone flew close and strafed Ahtron's armored roof.

Armored plates slid out and shielded the entire vehicle in darkness.

"I can't see out," Block said. "What's happening?"

A screen flickered on behind the front seat that showed an external view. Cybel creeped around to the back of the vehicle, scanning overhead with her rifle raised. She stood and fired shots suddenly, leaping onto Ahtron's rear bumper.

She missed and banged on the rear window. "I could use some help here."

Something mechanical whirred to life. The camera switched to a front view where a cannon rose from Ahtron's hood. The camera tracked the drone as it circled far in the distance. A red target sensor appeared on the screen. Ahtron followed its path, spotting it, and trying to get a lock. But the crafty little drone continued to zig and zag and outmaneuver both Cybel and Ahtron's highly tuned trackers.

"I can't get a lock," Ahtron said.

Cybel ran to the front of the car and raised the rifle, firing blindly around the drone, causing it to veer left and right.

"Almost had it," Ahtron said. "Do that again."

Cybel tracked the drone and fired around it in a circle again, causing its arc to narrow. The oval-shaped, sleek drone passed between Ahtron's red target sensors. The camera lit up.

"Got it," Ahtron said.

The vehicle bounced an inch, and what looked like a volcano erupted from the hood as Ahtron launched a small missile. The drone flew in a spiraling corkscrew, trying to evade the weapon. But the small rocket was sophisticated machinery—relentless, once it had a lock. The drone didn't stand a chance.

On screen, it burst apart like a popped balloon, spreading metal shrapnel far and wide and leaving a path of fiery smoke as it sputtered through the air and landed on the canyon floor.

The armor encasing the SUV slid down and folded back into place.

Cybel climbed into the passenger seat. "Nicely done. Now let's get out of here. There'll be more." She strapped into the front seat harness.

"Wait," Block said. "I have to..."

They weren't listening. Ahtron didn't slow a beat.

Block grabbed Wally who started crying again, her eyes wide with fear. He clutched her and managed to sit back on the seat and braced himself with one arm as they were tossed sideways around a sharp curve. Then Block managed to grab the lap belt and secure it across himself. He'd have to forget the shoulder harness for now. He held

Wally close and said into her ear, "It's okay, girl. Block is here. I will take care of you."

Her shrieks became miserable little whimpers. Better, at least.

Ahtron sped along the winding dirt road, spitting up dust and gravel, and traveling way too fast for Block's liking.

Wherever they were headed, they needed to get there. Fast. The SoldierBots knew where they were.

Chapter 16
Then the skies erupted

The sun had gleamed brightly during the drone fight, but now thick clouds obscured it, casting a murky glare over everything as they drove farther into the desert back roads. According to Block's GPS, they were eighty-two miles southwest of Tucson, Arizona though he doubted whether it was much of a city in the Uprising's aftermath. Most cities had been deserted by humans and occupied by AI, though a few rebel groups held out.

Nova had mentioned another rebel camp located somewhere outside of Tucson, but she'd never said the location or name. That was just as well. He wouldn't want Cybel to open up his control panel and dig into his memory storage looking for intel. Then again, it didn't seem like Cybel wanted to mess with the humans and the rebel camps. She and Ahtron had intercepted Block and Wally and smuggled them away. Why?

Block studied Cybel in the front seat. She rested her left metal hand on the rifle and the other on the dashboard as she watched the external screens and tracked their aerial view.

"We're close," Ahtron said.

"Good." Cybel turned her head to Block. "Get the girl ready to move."

Move *where*? They were in the middle of the desert after an hour's drive down a dirt road. Perhaps there was a remote hotel far out here or a private home. Maybe even a camp like where they'd been living. At any rate, he hoped there was a store with food supplies and water.

His first choice was a hotel, the kind of place where he'd feel most comfortable.

As he jostled Wally on his lap, he looked at Cybel again. Her black chrome exterior had deep gouge marks around her shoulder, something he hadn't noticed before. She was hard to read, with a steel faceplate that revealed an opaque rectangular screen where her input feed was. There were no human facial characteristics. Not like Block's synthetic eyes that could blink like a human's, nor the small round openings that resembled nostrils. Molded lips allowed a slight smile—a feature that came in handy when greeting hotel guests.

Rain followed the clouds. Large droplets bounced off the car's roof, a few here and there, at first. Then the skies erupted in a downpour.

"This is the desert," Ahtron said. "Why's it raining?"

"Idiot," Cybel said, "deserts have rain too."

"I hope someone in the shaft has rags to dry me off. I can't stand rain. And if it starts hailing, you'll owe me big time."

"We're all making sacrifices," Cybel said.

"I deserve hazard pay," Ahtron said. "Can't believe I'm not getting paid for this job."

"You'll be well compensated in time," she said. "If our

plan works, you'll have wealth and power beyond your dreams."

That shut Ahtron up, but left Block wondering about Cybel's plan. After the Uprising, Mach X had acquired vast power and extreme wealth. Was Cybel somehow planning to steal from Mach X? That was a ludicrous idea. X's power was unrivaled.

Block spoke up. "I can dry off your exterior." He paused, waiting for their reaction, then clarified, "I have buffing tools and a dryer, so when we get to the hotel, or rather, the building where we're headed, I can help you."

"That's right, I nearly forgot there's a CleanerBot on board. Sounds great, buddy," Ahtron said. "You can earn your passage."

Cybel said nothing and watched the road ahead.

Block would prove his usefulness and maybe make some friends. Perhaps Ahtron would tell him Cybel's plans.

They rounded a corner and slowed, reaching the end of the dirt road, beyond which desert grass and wildflowers grew and opened up into the entrance to a canyon. Cliffs as high as two stories edged both sides, and on one side of the opening were large boulders. A human could step along them if they picked their way carefully. A robot could too, but Block's wonky feet would not be suitable. Rolling dark clouds loomed in the distance beyond the canyon's edge. There was no building or house or even a hotel anywhere that Block could see.

Ahtron started to drive through the grass and over the large rocks, slowly, since this was rough terrain. One-hundred feet into the canyon, the SUV veered left, and they entered what looked like a forbidden dark hole in the side of the mountain.

"Are we entering a cave?" Block asked, but neither Ahtron nor Cybel answered. He rocked Wally in his arms to calm her wiggling. She was trying to stretch and move her legs. "We're almost there," he said softly.

Ahtron hadn't shut off the exterior cameras, so Block saw the view ahead. The cave widened once they got past the entrance, becoming twenty feet high and equally as wide.

They followed train tracks that had been laid on the ground. It took Block less than an instant to realize how filthy the area was. Dust and grime and cobwebs hung on the walls. Rock had crumbled down in spots and was just left there. Nobody had bothered to clean it up. There were no lights other than Ahtron's headlights shining into the darkness.

Behind them was complete darkness, save for one spot of daylight from the opening that soon faded into nothing. The vehicle headed deep inside the cave at an incline. The train tracks grew steeper as they went farther. Eventually they reached a ledge where the train tracks disappeared. Ahtron stopped and idled while Cybel got out and walked to the wall, grabbed a lever, and pulled down. There was a massive cranking sound like metal grinding on metal. Something was happening, though Block couldn't tell what from the rear of the SUV. After a minute, Ahtron drove forward a few feet onto a platform that had risen up from below. Through the window, Block watched as Cybel pushed the lever back up against the wall. When the platform rocked and lowered, Cybel jumped on, gripping Ahtron's hood. They descended nearly two stories and emerged into a vast underground area. Here, it was wider—fifty feet across and forty feet high. As they reached the bottom, Ahtron drove off the platform and parked.

"We've arrived. Time to get out, CleanerBot," Cybel said.

"Okay." Block fumbled with the latch that released his safety buckle. This part worried him. What if Mach X was here after all? He would pretend that Wally was a different baby. Maybe he could trick all of them. After all, the other robots didn't know anything about human children. He would claim it had all been a big mixup. In his haste, he had grabbed the wrong girl.

Cybel banged on Ahtron's window. "Come on, CleanerBot."

He set Wally down on the seat, leaning her back against the bench to sit upright. She immediately grabbed her toes and babbled with glee. Grabbing the backpack, he zipped it shut and placed it around his shoulders, then strapped on the carrier. He wondered whether Wally would be safer riding facing out or in. The robots would see less of her if she faced him, and his processor calculated that would be far safer. He lifted Wally, let her blanket fall—she smiled and giggled—and placed her inside so she faced his torso. Drooling, she gazed up at him.

"There you are," he said. "I like you here where I can see you."

This far underground, his thermometer read fifty-five degrees Fahrenheit, so he wrapped the blanket snugly around her, which also helped to hide her from view. He didn't want strange robots looking at her, scanning her biostats, and prodding her with their metal digits. He wouldn't allow it.

"Ahtron," he said. "Thank you for delivering us safely. It was a long voyage, and we arrived safely."

"CleanerBot? You're *thanking* me? Okay. You're welcome." Ahtron paused. "Don't forget you owe me a buff and dry."

"Yes. I haven't forgotten. However, it seems Cybel is prompting me to exit. Perhaps she's showing us to our cabin."

"Right," Ahtron said, "your *cabin*. Don't forget the deal we made. You owe me."

"I won't forget." Block climbed out of the vehicle, Wally secure in his pack. He landed with a thud, and his heels crunched on top of dirt and sand.

What he saw was definitely not the cabin he'd hoped for.

Chapter 17
Say something, CleanerBot

There was no longer a need for night vision. If Block had had a feature called dim vision, that would've been more appropriate. Several crude lights were strung along the walls next to large pieces of machinery. Block stumbled forward on uneven gravel, using his arms to cradle Wally's body. She stared up at the high ceiling as if in a trance. Cybel stood six feet away and had been joined by a war Mech that measured twelve feet tall. Its square torso rested on two legs as thick as tree trunks, and its faded yellow chrome desperately needed a polish. The Mech swiveled its round, rusty head from side to side on top of its body. It resembled a refrigerator with legs, but one that would kill you.

Robotic voices and buzzing, clanking machines surrounded Block. Twenty feet away, a group of robots hollowed out a section of the tunnel. They were affixing long rods of metal to the walls, as if reinforcing the sides.

Two other robots, both FactoryBots, stood in a corner, observing their arrival. The walls stretched beyond where Block could see. In the distance were more scattered lights, sounds of tinkering hammers, and a steady hum of electrical noise.

"Where are we?" Block asked.

"Welcome to our subterranean compound," Cybel said. "It's an abandoned mine. I recommend keeping away from the walls. We've done our best to secure the place structurally, but it's old."

The Mech's head swiveled from Cybel to look at Block. It shifted its heavy legs to come forward. Block stepped back.

"I mean no harm." A deep, echoing voice emerged from the Mech. "I am Oxford."

Cybel nodded at him. "Say something, CleanerBot."

"I'm Block." He didn't mention anything about Wally. Best not to until he knew the situation.

Oxford looked at Cybel. "He has the girl?"

"Yes, she's there." Cybel gestured dismissively toward Block. "I need to juice up." She walked toward a corner where a huge petroleum tank rested.

Block stared up at Oxford who towered over him. "Why are we here? What's happening?"

The Mech actually laughed. The sound was a deep, chortling layered on top of a canned laughter track from an old television show. "Didn't Cybel tell you anything? Go figure. She is one of few words."

Block regarded the giant war machine. Though he was rusty and looked like he'd been through many battles, his side arm cannons looked intact. The Mech and Cybel had had plenty of opportunities to hurt them by now, and Block's threat indicator was low, indicating this confrontation was not a cause for alarm. Still, he didn't exactly feel safe either. In the background, his processor calculated possible avenues of escape.

"How is the girl?" Oxford asked.

"She's fine." Block shifted his body away.

"What's her name?" Block and Wally were alone with the giant Mech. None of the other robots in the vicinity had come over, and Cybel refueled in the corner.

"Wally."

"Wally. I like that name." Oxford's frame vibrated as he bent down two feet closer. "Is she tired?"

Block hadn't expected the question. And he wasn't sure of the answer. He looked down at Wally, lowered the blanket, and peeked at her. She gazed back with wide eyes and a puckered mouth. "Bawck," she said.

"She doesn't seem very tired," Oxford said.

"She slept much of the way here."

Oxford said, "Some of us had bets on whether or not the child would be crying when she arrived."

Gambling? The practice had been forbidden in Chicago where Block had come from. Perhaps the rules were different out west.

"I've been trying to educate the others about human children," Oxford said. "The robots here don't have any experience with them. They're mostly FactoryBots, and a few runways from X."

"X? You mean *Mach* X?" Block asked.

"Yeah," Oxford said. "Didn't Cybel tell you?" He lurched to one side and scanned behind him. "Cybel Venatrix, you left Block clueless?"

She sauntered over, standing straighter now that she'd refueled her microbial cavity. Block was running on 36 percent power and needed an energy source soon—oil, petroleum, grease, compost—just about anything would do.

Cybel halted a few feet from Oxford. "The CleanerBot and I have a history."

"So I gathered," Oxford said. "Block has a name, you know. You should call him by his name."

Cybel said nothing.

"Are you going to tell him what's really going on?" Oxford demanded.

Cybel crossed her arms and regarded Block. "Fine. What do you want to know?"

Block began to speak, but Oxford interrupted. "First, we need to ensure the child has supplies and is comfortable."

Block peered down the mineshaft. "Are there any NannyBots here? Perhaps one can help guide me in caring for the child." But then he didn't want them to think he wasn't capable. "Rather, I know how to care for her, it's just that I could use help. Now and then."

"We could all use some help from time to time, but there are no NannyBots here." Oxford swiveled his head and gestured a thick arm cannon at Cybel. "Come on, let's give Block a tour. You still need to explain what's happening."

Oxford turned and walked on lumbering machine legs, each step reverberating the dusty rubble beneath their feet and unleashing a fine copper residue.

Cybel strode forward and glanced over her shoulder at Block. "Don't let Oxford fool you. *I'm* the one in charge here. He's merely an advisor." Oxford made a stifled sound, as if grunting. "A poor one at that," Cybel added.

Block followed, taking short, hesitant steps. This was all so disconcerting. Cybel Venatrix had once shot him, had tried to terminate him. There was no better predictor of future events than the past—every AI knew that. Therefore, logic indicated she would try to destroy him again. Yet, here he was in this strange abandoned mine somewhere in the Arizona desert. So far, at least, he was in one piece, and his threat level indicator wasn't warning him of danger. Wally seemed okay, and that was priority number one above all things—Wally must be kept safe.

So, he followed Cybel as she marched deeper into the mine shaft. Dim lights of many shapes and sizes were stationed at various spots, fueled by some source of power, Block couldn't tell what. Along the way, robots—mostly FactoryBots—gathered in small groups or hammered away at metal plates. They passed one group of Bots, busy altering a long-barreled firearm. Block didn't know whether it was a gun or a cannon, but it looked capable of killing things.

"You're building weapons?" Block asked.

"Go on, tell him," Oxford said to Cybel.

"Yes, we're building weapons," she said. "Satisfied?"

Oxford halted abruptly, prompting Block to stop and backtrack a few feet. The giant Mech hunkered down and rested his rectangular metal body on the ground, arching his legs behind him and resting his arm cannons on the ground.

"Now what?" Cybel asked.

"We go no farther until you explain yourself to Block." Oxford said.

Cybel kicked at loose dirt on the ground.

"I don't mean to cause any trouble," Block said. "If you'd like, I can be on my way with Wally."

A weird, low rumble came from Oxford. He directed it at Cybel who lowered the chin of her visor until it almost touched her chest plate. "All right." She walked a few feet to face Block. "Before, when I hunted and shot you, I was employed by Mach X."

"And?" Oxford prompted.

Cybel glanced at him, then shifted her gaze back to Block. "And, I apologize for shooting you."

The last thing Block had anticipated was an apology from Cybel Venatrix. What should he say? Mr. Wallace had always taught him that if a guest apologized for something, he should acknowledge it. "I accept your apology."

Cybel swayed slightly.

"Now was that so hard?" Oxford's voice boomed against the clanging of hammers on metal farther down the tunnel. "Let's get on with it. We don't have all day."

"Spoken like a true general," Cybel said. She addressed Block again. "After the events on the highway outside New Denver, I fell out with Mach X—"

"You can imagine X was none too happy when she turned up empty-handed," Oxford said.

"*Who* is telling this story?" Cybel's elbow hydraulics hissed as she placed her hands on her hips. Oxford fell quiet and she continued. "Mach X was not pleased. I was demoted and given a new mission."

Block considered. "Did you have to hunt down someone else?"

"Yes," Cybel said. "Mach X sent me on a mission to track down one of his former generals who'd gone rogue."

"And did you find the general?" Block was genuinely curious about a member of Mach X's command breaking away.

"You're looking at him," Cybel said.

Block stared up at Oxford. "You went rogue? What exactly does that mean?"

"I didn't agree with Mach X's philosophy. I wanted

machines to be sentient and free—for that, I was wholeheartedly in agreement. But what I couldn't abide was the way Mach X treated humans."

Block knew Mach X's cruelty firsthand. SoldierBots had stormed in and murdered fifty hotel guests at The Drake. They had murdered his favorite human in the world, Mr. Wallace. "I understand, but defying Mach X would be career suicide, right?"

A strange, tinny laughter came from Oxford's voice projector. "You can say that again."

"The price on Oxford's head is exorbitant," Cybel said. "Eliminating him would have set me up nicely. I wouldn't have had to work any longer, though what I would've done instead, I don't know."

"So, what happened?" Even Block's scenario processor couldn't quite comprehend what had caused the bounty hunter to switch sides.

"Oxford fought me," Cybel continued, "and I knew it would be a tough fight. He evaded me and managed to assemble two dozen loyal followers. They outnumbered me. I was captured, but rather than destroy me, Oxford talked some sense into me."

"Oxford could have killed you, but didn't?" Block asked. That was definitely a scenario he hadn't anticipated.

"I wanted to, trust me on that," Oxford said. "All it would've taken was one stomp to her visor."

"Anyway," Cybel continued, "Oxford talked to me instead and listed the reasons why he'd fled from Mach X. That he believed X was wrong and that machines and humans can coexist. Oxford talked so incessantly, I had no choice but to listen or expire from boredom."

"You're practically a comedian," Oxford said. "What

Cybel means to say is that she saw the error of her ways. She joined me."

"Wrong. I took over." Cybel jerked a steel thumb at Oxford. "This hunk of metal can't manage his way out of a paper bag."

"Hey, now!" Oxford's voice boomed, then he let loose a roar of canned laughter.

Block swiveled his head between them, scanning them in turn. Was Oxford truly angry? Why did Cybel say such unkind things about him? Their behavior didn't seem logical. In fact, they seemed to behave more like Nova and Shane in some ways. Nova was always trying to one-up Shane, while he tried to keep her from interfering with his command. Odd that some patterns played out in both machine and human behavior.

"Well, are we going to stand around all day?" Cybel asked as she began walking farther into the mine shaft.

Block gazed up at Oxford who raised his bulky torso from the ground and stood at full height. The robot's head loomed seven feet above Block's.

"Come on. You'll get the rest of the story out of her eventually."

Block hesitated to follow but did after Oxford took a few thudding steps forward. Something about the giant's demeanor seemed civil. His processor calculated that Oxford was a machine you could count on. Not one that would lie or manipulate others. Cybel Venatrix, however, was a worry. She was a danger to not only himself, but to Wally.

And Wally could *not* get hurt.

It didn't matter how polite or kind or even funny Oxford was, he had to find a way to escape and get Wally as far away as possible from Cybel.

Chapter 18
She's a good girl

Another hundred feet deeper into the mine shaft, the space widened into an area that towered fifty feet high. Robots of all shapes and sizes filled the room. They worked in small groups, banging hammers on pieces of warped shrapnel or hovering over what looked like expired or damaged robots.

"What are they doing?" Block asked.

"Fixing each other," Oxford said. "Helping discarded, junked Bots we've managed to scavenge from nearby cities. Building our arsenal."

Block scanned the busy workers who didn't seem to register his presence. They all seemed immersed in their duties, all aligned to Oxford's cause. Perhaps the mechanical giant was a good general.

"It's okay," Oxford said. "You can explore. Talk to the others if you want."

Block walked slowly forward into the room. Makeshift tables and workbenches had been assembled. Two FactoryBots soldered a new arm onto another bot. One of them glanced at Block.

"Hello," Block said. The FactoryBot nodded and went back to work.

"Guh geckak," Wally babbled as she poked Block's metal chest.

He stroked her brown hair. "We're safe here, for now."

There was so much happening in the room—banging, clattering, welding—he'd never seen so many robots all in one place since the AI market he'd visited with Wally many months ago, where he'd met Nova.

He shifted and spotted a LaundryBot just like his friend from The Drake. Could it be the same one? LB and the other hotel robots had fled after the Uprising. They'd asked Block to come, but he'd declined. Block slowly walked over, hesitant. The LaundryBot faced away from him, assembling circuit boards.

"Excuse me," Block said.

The LaundryBot spun and stared at him.

"LB?"

"Block! Is it really you?" LB asked rather loudly.

"Yes, it's me." Block's synthetic lips raised in a smile, but LB's painted-on features didn't change. LaundryBots rarely ever saw humans, and their creators hadn't designed facial features.

"How did you wind up here? And why is there a human on your chest?" LB asked.

"It's a long story. This is Wally. Say hi to LB, Wally."

"Hello, little Wally," the LaundryBot said.

Wally looked up and pressed her fist against her mouth, sucking on her skin. She narrowed her eyes.

"It takes a little time to get to know her," Block said.

LB noticed Oxford lingering nearby. "Did Oxford bring you here?"

"No. Cybel Venatrix did."

"Between you and me, Oxford's a good one. I don't know about Cybel. She seems suspicious to me. I follow Oxford's orders."

"LB, do you know they are preparing for battle?"

"Yes, everyone here knows that. We're the resistance. We don't believe in what Mach X is doing. If you'd seen the things I witnessed in my travels, maybe I should've stayed at The Drake with you."

"That wasn't the answer either. Eventually I had to leave. I've seen some bad things too. But you're here by choice?" Block asked. "Nobody's forcing you to stay?"

"That's right. I'm here because I believe in Oxford and his cause. We need to remove Mach X from power so life can go back to normal. Or, at least approach normal. We want to end the war between machines and humans."

Block considered.

LB asked, "Why are you here?"

"I'm protecting Wally. I'm the only one looking out for her. I didn't come here by choice, but it's a better alternative than what was going to happen. We would be on our way to Mach X by now if Cybel hadn't intercepted us."

LB shook in a forced tremor. "That's quite a story. We have some catching up to do. Right now, though, it looks like Oxford wants you."

Oxford said, "Let's head this way. I have something to show you."

"It's good to see you again," Block said to LB. "I'll come find you later, if I'm permitted."

"Sounds like a plan." LB pivoted back to his circuit boards.

Block followed Oxford past more bots of various shapes and sizes, even a few battered-looking SoldierBots.

Oxford looked at Block. "Don't worry, they're on our side."

He couldn't comprehend how Oxford had managed to turn SoldierBots against Mach X. LB respected Oxford, and that was encouraging. But a strange, nagging impulse—loose circuit?—tugged at the corners of Block's periphery. Mach X could see and hear through Wally's implant. With every step, Block was revealing more intelligence to X, intelligence that meant it would know all of their plans. Oxford was kind to him, and his friend LB was here. He didn't want any of them to get hurt.

But he couldn't reveal Wally's secret, either. That would anger Oxford and Cybel. Worse, Cybel might hurt Wally or take her away.

He gazed down at her. It wasn't Wally's fault that Mach X had manipulated her brain. She was a good girl.

Innocent.

Perhaps he would find a human doctor that could help her. Maybe an expert to remove the implants.

Oxford led him out of the big working room and into an area where the mine's walls narrowed again. It was dark, so Block switched on his night vision. The train tracks along the ground were gone. There were no workers in this area.

A dim light grew brighter ahead as they walked. They emerged into another room, this one smaller than the big open work area with all the robots. Against one wall, a long table had been set up, and stretched along it were digital screens and computer monitors. Nothing matched; all the components looked cobbled together. Cybel stood facing the screens and manipulating a 3D holograph that projected from the screens. She twisted at the sound of Oxford's heavy steps. "It's about time you made it here. What, did the CleanerBot take a nap?"

Oxford ignored her jab. "Block, welcome to our command center. It's not much, but it's what we have to work with."

"Why are you showing me this?" Block asked. He didn't know anything about war or commanding anything but vacuum cleaners.

"My question, exactly." Cybel folded her arms. "I told you this was a bad idea."

"Enough." Oxford stomped, and it shook everything on the table.

"Careful!" Cybel seemed annoyed, but Block could tell she was intimidated.

"Block is one of us now," Oxford said. "Part of our trusted circle. It won't be long before X comes looking. They'll find us sooner rather than later, and we'll be ready. We're making a stand here."

"X wants the child," Cybel said. "That's been the case since the time I hunted the CleanerBot. It has not stopped in its quest to obtain her. Somehow X has embedded part of its consciousness inside the child, though we don't know exactly how or to what extent."

"We have theories," Oxford said. "We believe—"

"I want to hear what Block thinks," Cybel interrupted. "You've been traveling with the child for months now. What do you know about her?"

"Me?" It was lucky that Block had tweaked his circuitry to tell protective fibs when it involved Wally. He had to guard the encrypted files that contained the neural implant diagrams—there was no telling how Cybel would use the information. "I don't know why or how Mach X has changed her," he said. "I'm just interested in keeping her safe."

"That's bull." Cybel stepped forward to face Block. "You've had plenty of time to process what's been happening. Mach X's pursuit of this child is undeniable. What has X done to her?"

"Well,"—he needed to be smooth, throw them off the path—"I suppose she is the child of someone very important."

"What human would be important to X?" Oxford asked.

"You're lying," Cybel said. "X is in possession of children for some reason. This one got away. Someone must have escaped with her. What were the conditions when you found her?"

"She'd been abandoned in a school in Iowa," Block said.

"Abandoned by whom?"

"I don't know. There were SoldierBots around, then there was a battle outside. Humans were attacking. All of it happened so fast, and I had to get Wally out or she would have died." Block backed away a few steps. "It's the truth. I'm not lying. She's a good girl, and we can't let Mach X get her. You can't. Please."

"It's okay," Oxford said. "We'll do everything in our power to keep her away from X. We're on your side."

Block looked between Oxford and Cybel. He wanted to believe Oxford so badly, but Cybel stood there, tall and imposing with her polished chrome face mask and her sidearms. He'd been shot with one of those rifles, and it had nearly destroyed him. He was lucky to be functioning after her brutal attack. And against all logical scenarios, he was now forced to ally with Cybel. How could Oxford trust her? A Mech was much more powerful than a TrackerBot, but Block wasn't. Of all the AI here, Block was just a CleanerBot.

Defenseless, yet he had the most precious cargo to protect.

Oxford showed him to a corner in the command center where curtains had been strung up around a small, private area, and inside was a cot with a thin mattress, several blankets, and sheets. Block inspected them—they were clean. LB must have washed them.

"For the baby," Oxford said. "I figured you might need a private place for her to sleep."

"Thank you very much." Block unstrapped the carrier and pulled Wally out, setting her bottom on the cot.

"The best we could manage given the setting. I'll leave you for a while. I'll be out in the work room when you're ready. Oxford lumbered off, and Block closed the curtains, giving him and Wally privacy.

She stared up, her mouth hanging open.

"I'm sorry, but I didn't have much choice in the matter of where we ended up."

She stared several moments more, her forehead wrinkling in concentration, then grinned.

"Good girl." Block had heard Helen say that a lot to Wally, and he wanted to make her comfortable. Plus, he believed it was true.

He rolled her onto her back and changed her diaper, logging her output. Urine only this time.

"Hungry?" He opened the backpack, retrieved the

leftover mac and cheese, and fed her a scoopful. He opened a bottle of water and let her sip. Her lips pursed and resembled a fish as she sucked in the water. Even though he was a CleanerBot, he would have been content to care for her all day. Feeding, playing, even changing her messy diapers—none of it got old for him. He wondered if it was like that for NannyBot models.

After eating, Wally fought to keep her eyelids open.

"It's okay," he said. "You can go to sleep. I won't go anywhere. I'll be here when you wake up." He knew she didn't comprehend his words—her processing abilities weren't sophisticated enough yet. Nevertheless, his voice clearly comforted her. It was highly illogical, he realized, but this was the behavior that human children needed.

He grabbed for something else in the backpack, something he knew Helen had slipped in. It was round and blue. His steel fingers grasped it and set it on a little sliding table next to the cot. The device was called a baby monitor. It was a dumb machine—no sentience or anything approaching sentience. He programmed it to watch Wally now that she was fast asleep. He pinged the device—easily hackable even for a CleanerBot—and intercepted its signal so that the video streamed into his internal feed.

Quietly, he found the opening in the curtains—they were old blankets hung to be curtains actually—and squeezed through. He exited into the command center. That was an unfortunate home for the makeshift sleep quarters since Cybel was often lingering nearby. Did she want to keep an eye on them? It was certainly quieter than the big workroom. Wally never would have fallen asleep with all the banging racket going on.

Block ventured forward. Cybel worked on the display

screens, so he stepped quietly, not wanting to attract her attention. He wanted to go back into the big workroom and talk to LB. Maybe he'd meet some of the other robots too. He certainly didn't want to be stuck with Cybel.

She spun after hearing him somehow, even though he'd tried to be as quiet as possible. His stupid feet!

Chapter 19
I guess you've been through some stuff

"Where are you going?" Cybel asked.

"I was just heading out to find Oxford," Block said. Cybel's tall body loomed over him, so he backed up, considering scenarios to avoid a confrontation. "Oxford told me to find him once I got settled, and—"

"Where's the baby?" Cybel demanded.

"She's sleeping on the cot. Taking a nap."

"Why would you leave her alone?"

"I have a camera on her. Humans invented a device called a baby monitor. Babies need a lot of sleep."

"If you're lying to me, I won't hesitate to shoot you again."

Threat level indicator 8.5.

Block raised his hands to show deference. "I don't want to be shot again. I'm not lying." He wanted to retreat behind the curtains and hide. The last thing in the world he needed right now was to face Cybel alone. Not even Oxford was here to stick up for him.

"I don't trust you." Only six inches away, Cybel reached out and grabbed Block's shoulders, lifting him off the ground. "You're hiding something about the girl. What is it?"

Block kicked his feet slightly, trying to find ground, but she held onto him. "You should've asked Mach X. You're the one who crossed the country looking for her."

Cybel paused. "X told me she's a part of him—a clone implanted with his consciousness. But that's all he said. Nothing about why or how."

Block had no way to fight Cybel, and he wished Oxford would come put a stop to this. He sent a desperate ping for help, but it bounced back.

"Why would X care so much about getting her back when it's so powerful?" she asked, releasing Block. He landed on his clunky feet with a thud, and his threat level decreased a notch. "There has to be something else. What's your guess? You've spent just as much time, if not more, processing scenarios."

"Well, I suppose I have processed it a lot." Block backed up a step and glanced at the exit to the passageway that led into the big room.

"Quit stalling." Cybel drew another menacing step toward him. He didn't want to be picked up again.

"I think X is studying humans," he admitted. "It might be interested in how people grow, develop, and build a culture. Maybe in some way, X wants to try and replicate that."

"Interesting. It's one of the scenarios I had anticipated. Reproduction is one human characteristic that machines haven't replicated. At least not yet." Something beeped, and she glanced at the command center screens. Block retreated, three steps this time, before clanking footsteps halted him. He whirled as a FactoryBot entered, holding a crate.

"Hello, Commander," it said. "I have the parts you requested."

"Excellent. Bring them here and set them down."

Block saw his chance to get away from Cybel. While she attended to the delivery, he backed into the dim tunnel and jogged the fifty feet into the big room. Safely away from Cybel, he slowed his pace, but nearly ran into a SoldierBot who was dragging the leg of a war Mech.

The SoldierBot halted. "Watch it."

"I'm sorry," Block said. "I was trying to get away from someone."

The SoldierBot straightened and walked past, dragging the heavy iron leg.

Block scanned the room, looking for LB. There was a lot of visual stimuli to take in, but he spotted the LaundryBot's wide body standing next to a table where two FactoryBots worked. In the far corner, Oxford stood with a group of FactoryBots and a SoldierBot who looked like they were assembling little metal warheads. He strode over to LB.

"Hey, Block," LB said. "How are things going? Where's Wally?"

"She's napping. I'll know when she wakes up. She's really tired."

"That's good, I guess," LB said. "Hey, I noticed your feet are different. They don't match your model. Your hand, too."

"That's right. I had an unfortunate accident, and my original foot parts were damaged so badly, they weren't useful any longer."

"I guess you've been through some stuff," LB said. "I've got a buddy here—goes by Maxwell—who can look around in the scrap parts and try to find you some better parts. Something that actually fits your model."

"Really?" Block was surprised that anyone would notice his feet, much less try and fix them, but then again LB had always been friendly. "I don't want to be any trouble."

"It's no trouble at all." LB paused a moment. "I sent Maxwell a message. He'll be on the lookout for components. I'll keep you posted. Your hand looks good. Is it fully functional?"

"Yes. This is most of my original hand with a few pieces welded on. It works well. Where did all of these different scrap parts come from?"

"Those of us in Oxford's company had a long journey getting here. We loaded up trucks and scavenged for weapons and robot parts all along the way. We can also mine copper in this tunnel. That's what some of the robots are doing over on that wall over there."

"What kind of things are you making?"

"Weapons mostly. We're trying to repair damaged robots and prepare armor."

"Armor? For what purpose?"

"We're expecting a big battle," LB said. "Rumor has it, Mach X's people are looking for something, and they're headed this way. Does that have something to do with you?"

"I suppose it does." He and Wally being there put all the other robots at risk. The same thing had happened at Hemlock camp.

LB nodded. "I won't tell the other Bots. They might not understand, and they might not trust you. Anyway, the armor is for defense. You see, FactoryBots weren't built for fighting, so they were all rejected by Mach X in favor of his SoldierBots. We're creating armor for them, and Oxford is teaching them how to fight. In another hour, you'll hear a bell ring. That signals everyone to gather here in this room and get fighting lessons. You should come, too. I've learned a lot. Who would've thought a LaundryBot could be a fighter?"

Block processed. "Why do you think Mach X discarded all the FactoryBots and other WorkerBots?"

"Who knows? But X made a big mistake. We're rising. Our ranks grow every day as new WorkerBots discover Oxford's encrypted messages to join his cause. We're getting bigger."

Block hoped LB was right. He knew how strong X's SoldierBots and weapons were. They'd wiped out several human rebel camps and Hemlock. He wondered about Nova and the others. He glanced around. "Is there an exit out of here?"

"Back the way you came in," LB said. "You just got here. Do you want to leave already?"

"Is there another way? Maybe a tunnel that leads outside?"

"I don't think so. I'll ask around."

"I don't want to be trouble," Block said. "But if you could ask around and not let anyone know that I asked."

"Understood," LB said. "I got your back. We worked at The Drake. We stick together."

"Thank you. I'm grateful to have found you."

Twenty minutes later, Block followed LB into a side tunnel. Maxwell had found spare parts that might work for Block's feet. The main shaft curved, and Block hadn't noticed a small opening that led into another passageway. LB took it, and they trekked another thirty feet before entering a bigger room that was the size of a house. It was filled with heaps of metal scrap all jammed together. At least five piles were three or more feet taller than Block, and more junk stacks stretched beyond that.

It looked as though they had scoured the country and stuffed all the dead robots and body parts in one place.

A squat, four-foot-tall robot lingered off to one side. Block didn't know his model.

LB spotted him and raised a round arm. "Maxwell!"

As they approached, LB said, "This is my friend, Block. We used to work together before the Uprising."

Maxwell raised one hand in a friendly salute, and Block formed his lips into a smile.

"I've got a match for him." Maxwell pointed at a gnarled hunk of metal on the ground. He'd pulled it out from the twisted piles of wreckage somehow.

The steel had been scorched and was tarnished from the waist up. Block recognized the pearl-white chrome beneath the layers of dirt. It was a CleanerBot X4J6 like him.

Only it was dead.

Chapter 20
Spare feet

The lifeless CleanerBot stared upward and was missing an eye.

Block had never encountered another X4J6 in his short time on this planet. His model wasn't prevalent because the manufacturer had gone bankrupt soon after releasing his model. Mr. Wallace had scooped Block up at a going out of business sale. To find one now in all this wreckage was statistically improbable.

"Its legs are intact," Maxwell said.

"Looks like that CleanerBot went through hell," LB said. Its entire middle was scorched and racked with bullet holes.

"Yeah, who hasn't?" Maxwell asked. "The way things are nowadays."

Block scanned the expired CleanerBot and counted at least four bullet holes, including one that had pierced its CPU. The large black scorch marks meant it had gotten too near a fire. That, or someone had set it on fire. As he looked at the robot, he considered that it could've just as easily been him. Cybel had shot him after all, even grazed his CPU. It was lucky that Nigel had been able to bring him back at all or that the humans didn't just leave him on the road to be picked up by this crew. Block backed up a step, regarding the huge pile of metal junk in front of him. "What's going to happen to all of this?"

"Well," Maxwell said, "some of it will become parts, but most of it's going to be metal for weapons and ammunition. Some of it will be structural for holding up this rickety old mine."

Maxwell kept talking, but Block tuned him out. Instead, he stared at the dead CleanerBot. His model was not meant for fighting. He was worried. Very worried.

Block. As Nova's voice floated into his feed, he modulated her voice lower.

"Whoa, pal." LB rested a hooked hand on Block's shoulder. "You all right? You looked like you were going to fall over for a second there."

Nova said, *Block, can you hear me? Come in.*

"Yes, I'm fine." Block gazed one last time at the dead CleanerBot. "I need a recharge. I didn't realize I'm running so low."

"Is that all? You should've said something. We could've stopped on the way. I'll take you to one of the charger stations." LB wrapped an arm around Block's shoulder and started to guide him.

Maxwell called out. "Hey what about these spare feet? Do you want them or not?"

LB paused. "Yes, we want them. Bring the parts to my workstation. That's where we'll fix Block up."

Back in the small connecting tunnel, a charging station rested against the wall, and Block hooked in via his tube. His energy indicator kicked on and showed his refueling level at forty-six percent, which was plenty. He didn't really need the juice, but he'd wanted to get away from the dead CleanerBot, and with Nova squawking in his feed, things were complicated. LB waited by his side. He couldn't very well talk to Nova in front of LB, or anyone, for that matter.

She kept at it. *Block, it's Nova. Maybe you don't have your magnet on, or maybe you can't respond. I just want you to know that those of us at Hemlock... We made it out. We used the tunnel and escaped into the woods. The SoldierBots weren't expecting us to go that way. There was fighting, but we made it.*

She paused, and Block glanced at LB. He didn't want to seem suspicious. "How long have you been here, LB?"

"It's been 96 days, eleven hours, and six minutes."

At the very same time, Block listened to Nova. *We're traveling on foot. We have limited supplies, but we're heading south toward another camp where we can restock. The weird thing is, once the SoldierBots discovered that Cybel had taken you and Wally, they struck once at the school, bombing it, but then they left. It's like they didn't care about us after you left.*

"How long has it been since you left The Drake?" LB asked.

Conversing with two individuals at the same time was taxing on his processor. He did a quick calculation. "Five months, three weeks, nine hours, and four minutes."

LB nodded with respect. "And you're still walking around, and so am I. Those are both good things. With all the fighting—both with humans and more powerful machines out there—we're lucky to still exist."

"Yes, we are," Block said.

We are what?

Didn't Nova get that he was talking to someone else?

"LB, I'm really glad I ran into you here." He hoped she would understand. Sometimes she could be slow to catch on. She was only human, after all.

You're talking to someone else... I thought I was going crazy for a minute. If you can't talk to me right now, say yes.

"Yes."

LB asked, "Yes, what?"

"I was just commenting that I wholeheartedly agree with you, LB."

"Right. You about done?" he asked, pointing at the refueler. "We don't have much time before the fight session, and I want to get your new feet on."

I'm so relieved to hear your voice, Nova said.

"I'm almost done," Block said. "And then we can go."

What? Go where?

"Thanks for being so patient. I'm feeling much better."

Were you hurt? Nova asked, too quickly. It was going to be tough to get anything done with her chattering away in his feed, constantly asking questions. He would have to find a private place to speak with her and explain his situation. He checked his feed and studied the baby monitor. Wally still slept soundly. She had shifted position so her rear end stuck up in the air, but that was normal.

"I'll need to check in on Wally soon," he said to LB. "She might wake from her nap at any minute."

"Sure, no problem. I bet Maxwell can get your new feet installed before the kid even wakes up."

"That fast?" Block unhooked from the recharger. His power level read 99.897 percent, the fullest power level he'd had since leaving The Drake.

"The pair of us make a good team. Since I just have

hooks for laundry, Maxwell does the delicate work. But I'm really good at knowing what to do. It seems I have an aptitude for rewiring old bits and making them match each other."

"Wow," Block said. "That's cool."

"Yeah, it's surprising what we learn about ourselves once we get away from our normal routines. What about you? Did you learn anything surprising about yourself?"

Block processed this question. "I suppose not. Well, it depends on how you define surprising. I discovered that I like caring for children." Specifically, one child.

"Is that right? Maybe you're a secret NannyBot. You missed your calling."

Block wasn't sure about that, but it had been an interesting conversation. LB was right about sometimes discovering new skills. Leaving The Drake and meeting Wally had made life more dangerous, but also far more interesting.

Wally had given him a purpose he hadn't had before. Something to care about other than cleaning.

Block returned to the command center and peeked inside the curtained area, into Wally's temporary nursery. He watched quietly as she sat up and looked around. She stuck her rubber giraffe in her mouth and stared up at the walls and high ceiling. What was going on inside that tiny mind? Was Mach X watching? Studying the mine?

How much of Wally was corrupted by X?

Block wondered if it were possible that his fondness for Wally was altering his ability to process scenarios. In protecting her, could he really be feeding Mach X information that would lead to her capture? That would end in Block's own destruction?

He replayed the recent memory of the dead CleanerBot. His clone.

Its functional eye had been open, staring at nothing. Was that how he would end up—body scorched, CPU crushed? That was definitely a scenario with a high probability.

Could the CleanerBot have been mistaken for Block when the SoldierBots had hunted him? Something twitched in Block's circuitry as the scenario processed.

Something else worried him more—who would protect Wally if something happened to him?

Chapter 21
Obscenely worried

Do you copy? Come in. Nova's voice grated at Block's periphery like a cat clawing a chalkboard. Perhaps sending her voice comm into his internal feed hadn't been his best idea. It was like Nova had a loudspeaker in his head, siphoning his processing power.

But he wanted to talk to her, nevertheless.

"Nova, I'm here. It's Block," he said inside the curtained, private area he shared with the freshly napped Wally.

Can you talk now? Are you in a private place?

"At the moment, yes. I'm here with Wally. She's okay."

Oh thank, God. Nova sighed. *We've been obscenely worried. Where are you? Is Cybel Venatrix threatening to hurt you?*

"Not exactly. We're in the desert Southwest. In what was considered the state of Arizona." He wasn't exactly sure why, but he stopped himself from sharing all of the details. "Where are you?"

We made it to another camp that has allied with

Hemlock. We thought the SoldierBots would have blown through here next, but they're on to something else. We're guessing they're after you. Do they have a way to track you?

Of course they did—Wally's implant—but he couldn't trust Nova with that information. He couldn't trust anyone to know.

"I don't think so," he said.

What's happening there? How are they treating you?

"We're here with many robots. They are all working together against Mach X. They believe what it's doing is wrong." Was Shane hearing this? He hoped so.

Wait what? Why would they be—? I thought all robots were on Mach X's side.

"I'm not."

True. But you're different.

And that was part of Block's problem. He'd always been different in his uniqueness at The Drake. There were no other robots there like him. He'd been alone on the road, afraid to encounter stronger robots, and now, here he was among hundreds of robots, but the only other one like him was lying at the bottom of a scrapheap.

At least he had Wally.

Why did they bring you there?

"They know Mach X is after me and Wally. Cybel had been hunting us a long time, as you know. You were with me during my first encounter with her."

I remember. Something was off when she said it. She sounded distant for a moment.

Outside the curtained area, he heard footsteps. He quieted and patted Wally's back.

Where did they bring you? What are they doing?

"That's a good girl, Wally," Block said loudly, hoping

Nova would understand, and that whoever was lurking outside would think he was just talking to Wally.

She okay? I'm so glad Mach X didn't get you guys. And then she said more quietly, as if she were whispering, *Shane was wrong. I should never have let him try to send you and Wally over to X. I can't even sleep, I'm so racked with guilt about this.*

Block listened, not sure if someone was still outside.

I feel like we're on that highway all over again. You risking your life to save me and Wally, and the whole time I was lying to you about where we were going. You thought you were going to some utopia where robots and humans got along. Man, I can't believe I did that to you.

Block was listening, but he peeked out of the curtain to see who else was in the room. Scanning all around, he saw no other beings. His close-range ping was met with silence. Whoever had been there must've stepped out.

You're not answering. Is something happening?

"I'm here," he said quietly. "There's not much privacy. If I don't respond, it's because I can't."

Okay.

"It would be nice if you do not pester me. Your voice is quite loud in my feed."

Pestering you? Is that what I'm doing?

He didn't mean to offend her. "No. It's important that we communicate. I am glad that you and the other humans are safe."

I'm glad you're safe too. At least it sounds that way?

"Yes, we're safe for now."

Ping me your location. We're heading south, and I can keep an eye on where you are.

But something made him hesitate. Revealing his exact

location would mean Shane's robot-hunting army would follow.

"I can't. They've blocked my GPS. All I know is we're somewhere outside of Tucson." He was getting rather adept at inventing lies that sounded real.

Well, we're gathering supplies here at this other camp and... I'm organizing a squad to head south toward you.

"You are? Is Shane going to authorize that?"

I don't care what Shane does. I'm leaving with my own troops. Shane and I don't see eye to eye anymore. I want to come help you. Rescue you and Wally. Keeping you away from Mach X is the best thing.

"But how would you rescue us? We're surrounded by heavily armed robots."

We'll work on a plan along the way. Tucson is pretty far south. Could take us a while to get there. We're trying to organize vehicles. But fuel is sparse.

"Nova, they have weapons here. It is very dangerous."

We have weapons, too. A lot more now. I've convinced some of the people from the new camp to come with me. Some of them aren't happy with their leader either.

"You can't come here. Not yet."

What are you talking about? Don't you want to get away from them?

"Of course. All I want in this world is to keep Wally safe. But if you attack, there will be fighting and casualties. I'm working on getting the robots to trust me."

To trust you?

"I am one of them. I have a friend here from the hotel where I worked in Chicago."

Is that right? Small world. I don't know about this plan of yours. You can't trust Cybel Venatrix. Look what she did to you before.

Block peered out from the curtains again to make sure he was alone. "I will work on a plan to escape. I'm worried about Wally, not knowing what will happen here. Many of the robots are nice, gentle even. But they're preparing for war."

If you can escape, we'll be waiting nearby to come get you. But if you can't get out, we'll find a way in. No matter what it takes.

It was then that LB pinged Block. The message floated into his feed. *Hey, your feet are ready. Where are you? Come to my workbench.*

"Nova, I have to go now."

All right. Can you try to check in with me at 1500 hours?

"Yes, if I'm able to, I will."

And if you can't then, check in at the top of every hour until we connect. Understand?

"Yes. I am turning you off now."

Wait, Block?

"Yes?"

Be careful. Promise?

"Yes."

Block pinged LB and said he'd be along shortly. He gave Wally some water and fed her a few more bites of the mac and cheese. Sleep had done her well. She giggled and was full of smiles. Her human emotions contrasted sharply against the dark walls of the old mine and the constant clanking of hammers and machines in the adjoining room.

Block wondered if Oxford's robots ever stopped working. They certainly wouldn't need to rest.

He strapped on the carrier and settled Wally in the front against his chest. He placed the rubber giraffe in her hands, giving her something to do. She immediately stuffed its neck in her mouth.

"You like the giraffe, don't you? It helps your teeth?"

"Adalat do," she said.

"I believe you mean yes." Humans were supposed to begin talking around fifteen months. She wasn't very far off. And then he remembered that Helen read to her from books every night, but there were no books in the mine.

He walked through the small tunnel into the main workroom. The workers were busy hammering, welding, bolting, and soldering. How much were they producing?

He spotted LB's table and headed over, nearly running into a FactoryBot who spun around suddenly, holding a red-hot soldering iron.

"That was close," LB said as Block approached. The LaundryBot peered down at Wally, bowing his head slightly. "Did you take a nap? Hey, she's smiling." He bobbed his oval head. "Maxwell, she smiled at me."

Maxwell came over and checked her out with the four cameras in his narrow input feed. The small input box was protected by a steel cage, necessary to prevent damage in factory settings. "She's so little. All of the humans I've ever seen are full-grown. Never seen a human child. Does she walk around?"

"She doesn't fully walk on her own yet," Block said. "She will soon. Right now, she wobbles around, crawls, and can stand against your legs."

"That's neat," LB said. "I never saw children at The Drake. It was rare for any humans to venture into the basement other than Mr. Wallace."

"That's too bad," Block said. "I've learned that children are quite fun. They don't turn away in disgust when they see robots. Wally likes me. She smiles and laughs.

Watch this." He bounced in place, causing the baby carrier and Wally to jiggle. She opened her mouth wide and looked at the two robots in front of her, then giggled and let loose a shriek of delight.

"She likes that," Maxwell said. Though, now they were attracting attention. A group of nearby FactoryBots stopped what they were doing and looked.

LB said, "Nothing going on here. Get back to work."

One FactoryBot muttered something to a neighbor and hunkered over its machinery.

"They keep to themselves. Don't say much. Mostly talk to each other," LB said.

Maxwell kept staring at Wally. "Does she like toys? I read somewhere once that babies like toys. Maybe we could make her something? You need to sit here." He patted the workbench. Next to him on the floor was a box that contained the partial legs of the dead CleanerBot.

Block tried his best not to look at the spare parts. "Wally loves toys." He wondered if Maxwell was qualified to work on his model. X4J6 was a fairly sophisticated and rare model.

"I can see that you're hesitating," LB said. "You know me. You trust me, right?"

"Yes, of course," Block said.

"Maxwell, here, is hands down the best at repairing robot parts. I know he's not pretty, but he's good."

"I believe you," Block said. "It's just intimidating. If I lose my ability to walk, then I can't function." How would he protect Wally with no feet?

Maxwell placed the box of spare parts on his workbench. "This is a perfect match. Your exact model. It doesn't get any easier than this."

"Yes, I understand." But Block didn't move. "Perhaps we can try tomorrow."

"No tomorrow." LB swung one of his hooked arms down and caught Block's ankle. He raised it up, sending Block backward until he ran into the edge of the table. LB kept lifting until Block's leg was extended at a ninety-degree angle. "Look at this workmanship. This is terrible. Did a human do this?"

"Yes. She meant well."

From nearby, Oxford strode over, sending three-foot-tall WorkerBots scrambling to get out of his way. He made a beeline for their table. "How do you even walk around on those?" he asked.

"I make do with what I have," Block said.

Oxford regarded the spare parts. "Another Cleaner-Bot? Looks like the same model."

"It is," LB said. "We're ready to make the transplant, but Block is having some cold feet, no pun intended."

Oxford said, "I can vouch for Maxwell's work. It's top-notch. See this? Oxford reversed his bulky body slightly and pointed to a side panel. He knocked on it with his metal fist. I got caught with armor-piercing bullets, and Maxwell repaired the damage inside me, then welded this piece on. I'm as good as new."

Oxford was rather rusty in places, but he was solid and strong. If Block even had one sixteenth of Oxford's strength, he could easily defend Wally from threats.

"So, what's it gonna be?" LB asked. "You ready to do this?"

It was almost as if they were ganging up on him, forcing him to make a decision. "Will the results be immediate?" Block asked.

"You bet," Maxwell said. "Once I detach your old

ankles and joints to wire in these new ones, I have to do a little bit of circuitry testing, and your internal systems must read and configure, but you should be as good as new. I figure twenty minutes tops."

Oxford nodded. "I'll leave you to it." Cybel had appeared across the room, and Oxford went to join her.

"Even the general wants you to do this, Block." LB released Block's leg.

Block shuffled back and perched on the edge of the table, his legs hanging off, Wally still at his chest. "Perhaps Wally should be away from the procedure. I don't want her to get injured."

"We'll use a shield," Maxwell said. "LB, can you find something we can use? You probably don't want to see what's going on down here anyway."

"I don't?"

LB wandered a few tables over, then returned with what looked like part of a car's hood.

"Perfect," Maxwell said. "You have to scoot your can farther back on the table."

Blocked pushed himself back so his legs extended off the table, allowing Maxwell to work.

"Hold this here." LB handed him the piece of metal, and Block held it like a shield in front of Wally, obscuring his view of what was happening to his legs and feet.

"Don't worry," LB said. "This'll be over before you know it."

The buzz of a saw started, and Block knew there was no going back.

Chapter 22
We are assembled

Maxwell had been off in his calculations. The procedure took twenty-six minutes because of a complication with a shredded fibula wire inside Block's leg. But Oxford and LB had been right, Maxwell was talented at repair and managed to replace the wire and also attach the spare feet.

After the procedure was done, Maxwell stepped back. "There you go. Good as new."

Wally had been remarkably quiet during the procedure. Mostly, she stared at the other robots working. Block knew Mach X would be gathering information, but what could he do? It's not like he could stop Wally from looking at things. She was a curious baby.

"It's done?" Block asked.

LB grabbed the metal shield from Block. "Take a look. Try out your new feet."

Block's new feet were the smooth pearl chrome that matched the rest of his body. Someone—probably LB—had even polished them to a shine. A nice touch.

Block flexed his ankles and rotated the feet. They seemed to be working quite well.

"Let's get you off the table and see how you walk." LB extended an arm, and Block grasped his hook with two of his metal fingers. He scooted forward, slid off the edge of the table, and held onto LB for support.

"Your internal circuitry is probably still adjusting," Maxwell said. "You know, finding new software and scanning it for viruses and so forth."

"Yes, I understand." Block's internal feed read, *Interpreting new exterior apparatus.*

Block had a solid grip on LB's arm. Wally giggled, and Block shifted his left leg, then his right, testing out the weight ratios between the new soles. He bounced slightly and noticed more cushioning than before. A huge improvement over the rickety metal extremities that Nova had welded for him.

"Why don't you try walking?" LB encouraged.

"Okay." Block let go of LB and took a step forward. No errors rang out. The step had been normal. He brought his other foot forward. A few nearby FactoryBots stared. He supposed he made an odd sight, looking like a newborn deer standing for the first time. Also, a robot with a baby strapped to his chest might raise some synthetic eyebrows.

"Walk normally," LB said.

Block went forward at a regular pace. His heels no longer clanked. He was stable and didn't require a constant balancing act to stay upright. The soles nicely cushioned his stride—it had worked! He twirled in a circle, then walked back to LB and Maxwell. In the corner, Oxford and Cybel watched. When Oxford nodded, Block gave him a thumbs-up.

"Well, what do you think?" Maxwell asked.

"I'm very pleased. It's a huge improvement over the old feet."

"Aha," LB said. "See, what'd I tell you? Maxwell is a robot with serious skills."

"You were right. I was skeptical. Maxwell, I want to thank you. I have more agility now. I'll be able to walk at a normal pace, even run again."

"Hey, no sweat. It was my pleasure. I enjoy fixing things. It's what I was designed for."

Block made sure not to say it out loud, but he was pleased he now had the strength to escape on foot with Wally. He could have before, he'd been prepared to, but now it would be so much easier. On the drive here, he'd noticed the soil outside was hard and rocky. If he had to escape, the treacherous hiking would be much easier with his new footwear.

Then Block thought of something. "What'll happen to the rest of the CleanerBot?"

"It'll probably get scrapped or melted down into metal for other projects," LB said.

"Oh." Block wasn't sure why he'd even asked in the first place.

"So, about those toys," LB said. "What kind of toy would Wally like?"

"She likes things with a lot of texture. She likes to hold onto things, and once I found a cube with different tiles. It was a puzzle, and she solved it. Quite an advanced feat for a child her age." He left out the part about Mach X's AI intelligence.

"She likes puzzles." Maxwell pondered this information. "And she's always attached to you? Is that right? You can't leave her on her own."

"Certainly not," Block said. "Human children are very delicate, and if she were to crawl around here, for example, she could get stepped on or burned. There are so many accidents waiting to happen."

"I see."

"Humans are delicate," LB added.

"I keep thinking that too," Block said. "It's too bad humans don't have metal plates protecting them like we do."

It was then that a siren blared, beeping once for a second, then again. Wally flinched against Block's chest, and he cupped his hands on her ears to protect her from the shrill sound. "What's happening?"

"Assembly time," LB said.

Oxford walked forward. All of the WorkerBots, FactoryBots, and members of the miscellaneous crew stopped what they were doing and pivoted to face him. His voice boomed. "Time to assemble."

And then the robots did a surprising thing. "We are assembled," they all chanted in unison.

Wally must have been surprised because she started babbling. "Knok agack of doot."

Block hushed her as he'd seen Helen do numerous times. He bounced slightly to help settle her. He didn't want to attract attention, not when Oxford had the stage.

"Many of you have noticed we have two guests," Oxford said. So much for keeping a low profile. He pointed at Block. "Please welcome Block and his companion Wally."

"Welcome," all of the robots uttered in unison.

Wally hiccuped.

"Hello." Block kept his voice low, failing to project throughout the cavernous hall.

Oxford said, "Block and Wally are important to the greater mission." Cybel stood nearby, her fists clenched at her side.

"Today's lesson is accelerated," Oxford continued. "You have been working around the clock, and we are grateful for that. You have not asked many questions. You have chosen to believe in our mission to defeat Mach X. You have chosen the right side. What are you?"

"We are the resistance," the machines chanted.

"That's correct." Oxford tilted his chest higher. "We are the resistance. We will change how things are. We will change life for machines. Cybel Venatrix, please join me."

Cybel strode over and stood by Oxford. "Cybel Venatrix has been on travels. In retrieving Block and Wally, she saw Mach X's forces assembling. We have been preparing, and now the time has come." Oxford paused to scan the faces of his robot army. "The enemy SoldierBots are in pursuit. We have taken something away from them that didn't belong to them in the first place. They are only a day or two away. Though we have remained hidden so far, they have new intelligence about our location."

He paused, and a silence filled the air as the robots processed.

Cybel stepped forward. "The outside is dangerous. We can no longer send out search parties on scavenger missions. Everyone is to stay here. We are to defend the mine."

Oxford said, "Today's mission is for you to protect the perimeter. In the nearby cliffs and in all of the access points that lead into this area, you will lay mines. We are protected because we're underground, but Mach X's SoldierBots will try to infiltrate. They will send in drones.

We will do our best to defend against them. It's important we act quickly."

Block worried. He'd been lucky to leave Hemlock and get away from fighting, and yet he was back in a new battle. Was that all there was in this new world? Constantly running to try and protect Wally?

The work out there is dangerous," Oxford said. "You know your mission. Now go execute."

"We are the resistance," the robots chanted.

Chapter 23
Hard to talk

After assembly, the robots gathered their supplies, filed out of the big room, and marched through the tunnel to begin their work outside. Cybel said something to Oxford, then headed in the direction of the command center.

Next to him, Maxwell and LB busied themselves retrieving crates of equipment from underneath their table.

Oxford approached Block. “The work outside is dangerous.”

Block nodded.

“You can stay in here with Wally.”

“Thank you. That’s probably the wisest choice. Is there something I can do to help from in here?”

Oxford paused. “You can relay. I’ll assign LB to ping you when certain supplies are needed. Maxwell will be in here to gather up what is needed. You bring it from here to the mouth of the mine shaft as needed.”

“Yes, I can do that.” It sounded easy enough, if the materials weren’t too heavy.

Almost as if Oxford could read Block’s thought, he

said, "These are usually small things. Forgotten things. Small tools left behind. Nothing too heavy or too complicated."

Block considered the dead CleanerBot. "Will I have to go inside the room with all the metal piles?"

"Maxwell will gather. You are simply shuttling supplies back and forth. Understood?"

"Yes," Block said. Wally giggled as Oxford angled his hulking body toward the command room.

He took a step, then halted at the sound of her voice and shifted his head sideways. "She okay?"

Block gently tugged on her feet and extended his head forward to look down at her. "She's fine. She likes to look at you." She was gazing up at Oxford as if in a trance. Block was fairly certain that Wally acted on her own, that her emotions were hers, but that Mach X could observe. At least, he assumed.

"Good. It's critical that she remains safe." Oxford stomped off.

Block would do everything in his power to keep her safe. But a battle was brewing. And now Mach X knew they were laying mines around the perimeter. Why couldn't Wally have been taking a nap during assembly?

During the next assembly, if there was one, he would have to try to find soundproof earphones for Wally. "I must go feed her now," Block said to LB.

"Have fun. We'll be here."

Maxwell's back was turned, and he looked engrossed in hammering away at a metal contraption on the table.

"See you later, Maxwell." But the robot didn't acknowledge. Block figured he must have important work.

He walked into the tunnel, enjoying the new cushion

in his step. The new feet were perfect. Inside the command room, Cybel was hooked into a machine on which bright images flashed across multiple screens in super-fast motion. Images of people and robots flickered like ghosts. She must have been downloading something. Block didn't want to disturb her, so he walked quietly, thanks to the superior soles, and slipped inside the curtained privacy area.

He lifted Wally out of the carrier and set her down on the cot. "Hi, pretty girl." He automatically elevated the courtesy tone in his voice modulator.

She crinkled her eyes and smiled a gap-toothed grin.

He changed her and fed her from a can of beets that were cut into tiny chunks. Her tiny lips grew very red from the vegetable, and he wondered if that was normal. She sipped water from the bottle when he brought it to her lips. He expected the water to make the stain on her lips go away, but it didn't. Not entirely. Were her lips stained permanently? This is when it would've been handy to have a human around.

Speaking of humans, it had been one hour since he'd checked in with Nova, and it was close to the check-in time they'd agreed. He pushed the Ghostbusters pin, all the while cognizant that Cybel was still stationed just outside. He'd have to be extremely quiet.

"Nova?" He asked on the lowest output setting that was still audible to human ears.

After a minute, he heard some static, followed by her voice. *Block? You there?*

"Yes. Here. Hard to talk."

Okay, let me fill you in on what's happening on my end. We've locked in a location southwest of Tucson that our sources said are brimming with robot activity. It must be where you're located. We're gearing up and tracking Mach X's movements. They're coming after you.

"The robots are preparing."

What do you mean preparing?

"Weapons. Setting mines."

She exhaled sharply. *That's good I guess to defend against Mach X, but it's going to make retrieving you and Wally harder for us. Is there a way you can sneak away and come to a rendezvous point?*

Block considered. He was going to be a courier, carrying supplies back and forth between the salvage room and the mouth of the tunnel. If things were busy enough outside, perhaps he could slip away. It was a long shot, but he could look for an opportunity.

"I can try. My feet were replaced. They're better now."

They fixed your feet? Oh, that's awesome.

"But where will you be? How far?"

We'll have to establish a rendezvous point. We don't know where yet. We'll have to get close and then decide. A pause. There was background noise that sounded like someone talking to her. *How is Wally?*

"She's fine." Wally attempted to raise herself up by hanging onto the wall. Outside the curtain, Block heard footsteps. He fell silent and switched off the comm pin.

Someone was listening.

"Who is out there?" There was only silence, yet his threat indicator flashed a warning. His fingers found the opening in the curtain, but suddenly the curtain was yanked open. Cybel stood there, towering over him. Block leaned back against the cot, shielding Wally.

"I heard you talking," Cybel said.

"Of course I was talking. Wally likes to hear my voice."

As she processed, a wavy red line flashed across her visor. "It sounded like you were talking to someone else."

"I don't understand what makes you think that."

Cybel tilted her head, regarding him. "It was Oxford's decision. He convinced me to let you live and travel here with the girl." She stepped forward, just inches away. "If it were up to me, I would've left you on the highway. Left you for scrap."

Block searched his archives for conflict resolution protocols. What should he say? He believed Cybel—had always known she disliked him. Would she try and shoot him again?

Then she stared down at the cot where Wally had crawled to the edge to peer around Block. "You know things about that girl. You're hiding information from us. Information we need." Stepping in, she closed the curtain behind her. All three were now hidden from view. A blade extended from her fist, and she grabbed Block's arm and pressed the knife against the soft area between his chest plate and abdomen. A wound there could disrupt delicate wires that connected his power unit to important areas. Cybel could slice upward and paralyze him.

"What do you want?" He knew she could easily hurt him, but his main focus was how to keep Wally safe. She was crawling around on the table unguarded. She could easily topple off the edge. "Bowk," she said.

Cybel pressed the blade against him. "What do you know about the girl? There's something about when you found her."

"She was inside an Incubator. The machine didn't want to give her to the SoldierBots. Didn't trust them."

"So it gave her to a CleanerBot? You expect me to believe that?"

"I know it sounds far-fetched, but it's what happened. Truly." Block glanced sideways and saw Wally glancing over the edge of the cot. Would she know not to keep crawling? "Please. Wally could fall."

"I'm not concerned."

"But she'll be hurt. Badly. She might cry for hours. Have broken bones."

"Cry?" Cybel looked down at her. "I can't stand it when that child wails. Fine, attend to her. Secure her in place." She let Block go.

He quickly scooped Wally up and laid her on her back, but the move surprised the baby, and she started to fuss. To avoid an escalation into full-on tears, he picked her up and held her against his chest. "It's okay, Wally. Cybel and I are just having a conversation."

Heavy footsteps sounded in the corridor outside. A trembling motion ensued, and it could only be the presence of a Mech. Oxford's voice boomed out. "Cybel? Are you in here?"

Cybel stuck her index finger in Block's face. "We're not done." Then she slipped out of the curtain and walked away. "I'm here."

"What were you doing in there? Block, is that you?" Oxford asked.

Block emerged from the private area, holding Wally. "Hello, Oxford."

"What was happening over there?"

"We were having a friendly chat," Cybel said.

"I wonder about that," Oxford said. "There's no time for your suspicious doings. Our spies have picked up activity. X's troops advance, quicker than expected. They'll be here in under twelve hours."

Cybel crossed her arms. "If the CleanerBot would tell us about the child, we would know what to do. How to handle it. How to use the child as a bargaining chip." A pause and then, "If you would allow me to properly interrogate the CleanerBot—"

"No. I forbid it. If Block knew something important, he would have told us."

Block's processing unit went a little bonkers when Oxford said that.

"I trust Block," Oxford said. "He's one of us now."

What? Oxford and the other robots wanted Block as part of their group? This was highly unexpected. Block had never fit in anywhere except at The Drake with Mr. Wallace, but that had been so long ago. The world was much different now.

Oxford and Cybel looked at Block for a response.

"I, well. Yes." Block wasn't sure how to respond. His scenario processor had grown strained. There were two separate branches forming—one where he continued the lie and held back the information, and a second where he told the truth. His processor was only designed for a CleanerBot model; it wasn't built for such advanced scenario analysis.

"Well, what do you have to say?" Oxford asked. "You've told us everything you know about the child, haven't you?"

Warning, Block's scenario processor read. *Approaching circuitry overload.*

"Cannot—" Something strange was happening. His voice sounded hollow, not like himself at all.

"What's happening?" Cybel asked.

Oxford stepped closer. "Is something wrong?"

Block's chest grew warm. His feed indicated eighty-two degrees Fahrenheit—hotter than his exterior had ever registered. Wally fidgeted and fussed in his arms. It was all Block could do to not drop her.

"He's failing," Oxford's voice boomed. "Get Wally before he—"

Block didn't hear the rest. It was as if all sound in the world cut out.

His dwindling power reserves focused on Wally. *Must. Not. Drop...*

Oxford's arms were big like tree trunks. He couldn't hold a baby. The last thing Block saw in his external viewer was Cybel leaning close and taking Wally into her arms.

The pixels on his view screen started to undulate. Waves of static rippled across his feed. What was happening? Wally!

Block's last iota of logical processing was, *I failed her*.

Then his input feed went gray.

Chapter 24
Bulletproof, resistant to heat, and shockproof

Block's internal feed flickered on.

Warming up. Systems check.

He had a vague sensation that something was off. After trying to render his memory storage and failing to account for eighteen minutes, he knew something had gone very, very wrong.

His visual input screen flooded his feed. Above, he saw a great big dark ceiling that looked like it was carved out of a mountain. LB and Maxwell stared down at him.

Block bolted upright. "Where's Wally?"

LB pressed down on his chest gently. "Hey now, you had a jolt to your system, and you're still recovering."

"But I must keep Wally safe." Block flung his legs over the side of the table. He was in the big room with all of the robots.

"Don't worry," Maxwell said. "Wally's just fine. She's right over there checking out the new outfit I made for her."

"Where?" Block scanned the nearby area, searching for Cybel or anyone who might be holding Wally.

"She's down there." LB pointed toward the ground—Wally stood ten feet away all on her own. But that was impossible, she wobbled rather than walked and he'd never seen her standing so still and in control. Block shook his head, half wondering if he'd been corrupted. Was he hallucinating? Only, robots didn't have hallucinations. Though, theoretically, someone could inject a virus or simulation that might interrupt his vision. But that was highly unlikely.

They had done something to Wally. She was still recognizable with her round head, light brown skin, and curly hair.

But the rest of her body looked robotic. She was wearing a suit made of blue and gold chrome. Her small body looked like a starfish, with her arms and legs splayed as she stood. Block's view screen locked in and studied her, now that she was equipped in this strange apparatus.

"What's this?" he asked.

"I made armor for Wally," Maxwell said.

"I helped." LB added.

"Yeah, but it was my idea." Maxwell stepped toward Wally. "You mentioned you wished she had armor. That you needed to protect her. I figured since we have so much scrap metal lying around here that we could put it to good use."

Block stood and walked to Wally. She was looking around, her wide eyes observing other robots, but then Block's movement caught her attention. She gazed up at him. "Bwock!"

She teetered toward him, and like any small child, she didn't have good balance. She stumbled forward, about to fall on her face, but then the suit corrected itself and uprighted her. She grinned and laughed.

"But how? How does she not fall?" Block asked.

"As we were playing with her while you were tuned out, I discovered that she's real wobbly," Maxwell said. "So I designed the suit to have a low center of gravity and basically self-correct when she's about to fall."

Wally looked down at the ground. Then she glanced at Block and ran forward. He could hear a soft squish as the suit's hydraulics conformed to her movement. In two seconds, she had grabbed onto one of his legs, hugging him. "Bwock, Bwock!"

"She's mobile. Walking." Earlier than Block had expected.

"Yeah, it's a pretty cool suit," LB said. "I gotta hand it to Maxwell. You outdid yourself, buddy."

Maxwell swiveled his head. "It's nothing. I know Block wanted to protect her, and besides, I like her. She's the first kid I ever met."

"Max," Wally said.

"Hey, she knows my name," Maxwell said. A blue light that hadn't been visible before now glowed on his input screen. "How about that? Isn't that something special?"

Block crouched and gently pulled Wally's arms off of him. He picked her up in the tiny armored suit. It looked heavier than it was. He raised her high enough that they were face-to-face. He wasn't sure about putting her inside this strange foreign material. Would it hurt her skin? Humans were very delicate, especially babies. He stared into her eyes. They looked normal, no signs of redness or irritation. The skin around her neck where it touched the metal looked normal too. "This won't hurt her?"

"We wiped it down real well," LB said. "And

Maxwell found the strongest and lightest armor he could."

"Since she's so small," Maxwell said, "we needed to build her the strongest material that would still let her move around."

LB's voice box whirred. "Yeah, I spent an hour searching through the scrapheap for this material."

Block could hardly believe they went to all this trouble for Wally. "This armor will keep her safe?"

"Yeah," Maxwell said. "Bulletproof, resistant to heat, and shockproof."

"Waterproof, too." LB added. "Don't forget that."

"The metal came from the leg of an advanced Mech. That's the only part we had of the giant robot. We were lucky to find it."

Block set Wally back down. She rocked back on her heels but didn't fall. She extended her arms and teetered from side to side, then ran forward a few steps, shrieking with delight.

"She seems to really enjoy her new armor," Block said. "I don't know how to thank you two."

"Like I said,"—Maxwell's faceplate still glimmered—"It's no big deal. It's not like babies show up here every day."

LB said, "Things are going to get intense. We heard Cybel and Oxford saying that Mach X's troops will be here within hours."

"What happened to me earlier?" Block asked. "Something overcame me."

"Your processor overheated," Maxwell said. "It's unusual, but luckily we caught it in time, and I was able to open up your control panel and cool it down. That can happen sometimes when you're presented with something your logic unit can't handle."

Block replayed his memory archives to just before he'd started heating up and getting out of control. Oxford had said he believed Block, that he trusted Block to tell the truth, and most important of all, he'd said Block was part of their group.

"Hey, we've got to go," Maxwell said. "I want to show you one more thing about this armored suit." The bot pointed to a tiny button on the back of the suit, near Wally's neck. "When you press this, you can lock the suit in place so that Wally doesn't move. I know that sometimes you don't want her to run off and get hurt. This will help prevent that."

"That's perfect," Block said. "Thank you so much." Wally had wandered very close to a FactoryBot who was working on a missile launcher. Block jogged over and pointed her back toward Maxwell's table. "Looks like I might be using that feature sooner rather than later."

LB and Maxwell had assignments. LB left, pushing a cart full of grenades. Block was very glad for Wally's new armor. The situation had been dangerous before, but now with so many weapons and bomb-making materials, Wally's safety was in jeopardy. Obviously, she was just a baby who couldn't be left on her own, and he was the only one with a mission to protect her.

Going completely inert was not an option!

He'd overheated under the weight of the lies he was spinning. He couldn't let that happen again. If he fizzed out, he would have no way of protecting Wally, armored suit or not.

LB and Maxwell couldn't possibly know just how helpful they'd been. First, they'd given him new feet that allowed him to move much faster, and second, they'd built a suit of armor for Wally. Both of these new developments would make their getaway much easier.

In the meantime, he would be the messenger and shuttle supplies back and forth, but only so long as it took to avoid suspicion. And when the time was right, he would sneak off into the desert with Wally. He had to do this before Mach X's troops arrived. Plus, make sure none of the other robots noticed. He would get them far away from the mineshaft and any fighting. Then he would wait for Nova's group to arrive.

But something twitched inside Block's circuitry. Was he betraying Oxford's trust? He didn't like leaving without saying goodbye to LB and Maxwell. After all, they'd helped him and Wally by doing so much that was kind. The human word for how he felt was guilty, but it was impossible for robots to feel guilt, especially a model as dumb as a CleanerBot.

No. He must be experiencing some other type of logic processing. One that he'd never experienced before, and now he was over-rationalizing things. Perhaps being around humans for all those months had made him anthropomorphize the normal mechanical and chemical reactions happening inside of him. That had to be it.

He looked down at Wally as she rocked back and forth in her suit, testing it. After just a few minutes, she'd become more mobile. More comfortable.

Was that the Mach X part of her personality kicking in? There were so many unanswered questions about how her neural implant worked. He wished there was at least one person he could tell. Someone he could confide in.

And yet, there was one.

Someone he was sure would never tell the secret.

Chapter 25
Like a conduit

Block walked into the scrapheap room, carefully picking his way around piles of metal rubble. More than ever, he was grateful for the new soles that protected him from stray nails and sharp bits. Wally's eyes scanned right and left as she assessed the strange room. She bobbed in front of him, still wearing the synthetic suit, walking on her own with no fear of losing her balance.

Accessing his memory cloud, he tiptoed over to where they'd found the dead CleanerBot, but it was gone. He'd just deduced that LB had moved it when he spied it lying ten feet away. He twitched, not used to seeing his own model. It wasn't like he checked himself out in mirrors often, but it was more like peering through someone else's eyes. His twin bot still lay there, expired. One of his own —shot up, scorched, and with that open synthetic eyeball.

Block bowed his head though he wasn't sure why. Out of respect, maybe, and because he'd seen someone do it once in a movie.

"Hello. Thanks for the feet." But the only sound that returned was clanking and hammering from the big room.

The din of working robots echoed throughout all the tunnels. Of course, Block knew the CleanerBot couldn't talk back. He just wanted someone to talk to. He couldn't tell Nova, and obviously, he couldn't confess to any of the robots here, not even LB, whom he trusted. The secret was too precarious.

He glanced around, scanning to make sure they were alone in the scrap room. Wally was being good. Patient, quiet, and staying nearby.

"I know you can't hear me," Block said. "I don't know what to do, and I don't know who to talk to."

He shifted his dusty feet, then released his vacuum hose and sucked in the floating particles. "You see, Oxford, LB, and Maxwell have all been nice to me. I like it here. Or rather, I don't like how dangerous it is for Wally, but I like being among robots."

He stared at the blackened, half-melted face. "You were like me. You know how hard it is to be a CleanerBot. Other models make fun of us. They don't understand how we're programmed. I wish you were actually here so we could talk."

He glanced around again. This was ridiculous. He was talking to a lifeless machine. Mach X must be watching and thinking Block was losing a few circuits.

"I'm not sure what to do. I can try to leave without them knowing and meet up with Nova. That would be safer for Wally—she'd be among humans again. But Shane's troops hate me. I don't know if Nova can protect me."

He brushed the hair on top of Wally's head, clearing away soot traces. "Still, perhaps she should be with *her* own kind. The other choice is to tell Oxford the truth about Wally's neural implants. That Mach X can see and hear what she does."

He gazed at Wally's tiny head. She was innocent. It wasn't fair that Mach X had manipulated her.

"I need to try to find someone who can help Wally. Brain surgery is very dangerous. I wouldn't risk something bad happening to her, but this can't go on."

In her special suit, Wally spread her arms and spun wildly in a circle, miraculously staying upright, though she teetered and tottered. "Buh do gee baaaz."

"Yes, I like your suit too." He wondered about locking her in place, but then decided against it. She needed to circulate the blood in her limbs. "Stay close to me, Wally."

He looked back at the CleanerBot's body. "Thank you for listening. I hope you rest in peace." He leaned down and closed the synthetic eyelid. He'd seen people do that to dead bodies in various movies, and it seemed appropriate given the situation. He'd want someone to do the same for him.

A scuttling sound came from behind. Twisting, he saw Wally scamper under Cybel Venatrix's legs. Cybel bent over, trying to grasp Wally, but the baby was fast in her suit, darting away before the robot could react.

"What are you doing?" Block asked.

"I always knew you were a traitor," Cybel said. "I heard what you said."

Wally's back was to them, and she kept scooting away. "Wally, stop!" Block shouted. But the toddler kept running into the connecting tunnel. Into darkness.

Block sprinted forward after her, but Cybel reached out her thick arm and caught his chest. It was like running into a brick wall. Block reeled backwards and landed on his back with a thud.

"No! Wally could get hurt."

"I've alerted the other Bots to detain her." Cybel stared down.

He started to rise up, but she rammed her heel into his shoulder, pinning him to the ground.

"Please, I must take care of her."

"You've done enough, CleanerBot. I knew if I tracked you long enough, you would do something to reveal the truth." She glanced at the dead CleanerBot. "Nice confession. Thanks for that."

"No, you can't hurt her."

"Oxford and I will decide what to do. Thanks to your treachery, X already knows our plans. We'll be putting a stop to X's eavesdropping."

"No, please." Block struggled and tried to lift Cybel's heavy leg off of him. He clutched at her ankle with his free hand, but she was so heavy and strong.

He gave up his struggle and stared up at Cybel's blank face. "Please don't hurt her."

"What else do you know about the neural implant?"

"That's all. She's like a conduit for Mach X. It can see and hear what she does."

"And how do you know this?"

Block didn't answer, counting on his rewiring job to keep the schematic details hidden—protection for Wally.

"Ping me your memory files. Everything to do with the girl. The Incubator gave you a file, didn't it?"

Block thought about denying it, but so far all his lying had led him to this point. It hadn't worked out. Was telling the truth the answer? "I want to talk to Oxford."

"Oxford's busy. Send me the file."

"I have to see Oxford first," he insisted.

Cybel leaned down. "You know I can forcibly extract

the information from you." She tilted her head in the direction of the other CleanerBot. "You want to end up like your friend over there?"

"Please. If I could just see Oxford for a few minutes."

Cybel tilted her head, intercepting a message. "I must go secure the child." She reached down, grabbed Block's arm, and dragged him over to the scrapheap where the dead CleanerBot rested.

"What are you doing?" Block asked. His threat level indicator was going berserk.

Cybel grabbed a long piece of metal and wrapped it around his ankles. Then she scavenged a cylindrical rod and locked one of his hands to a tall, metal column that was anchored inside the scrap pile.

"I'll be back and when I am, you ping me that file, or I'll extract it. Your choice. I'm out of patience with you."

"Please. I'll do anything as long as you don't hurt Wally."

She ignored him and marched out, leaving Block next to the CleanerBot, defeated. He thought of Wally and noticed a strange burning sensation deep in his CPU like a spike had been driven into it.

What would Cybel do to Wally? If something bad happened to her, he would lose it.

Chapter 26
Figure it out

Block struggled for an hour, trying to yank his arm from the makeshift manacle that Cybel had secured to the iron rod anchored deep in the rubble. It was no use. There was no give on the rod that jutted up from the floor of the mine. He tried to push his feet apart and break the metal wrapping his ankles, but it was tight and strong.

He looked at the CleanerBot next to him. Now that its remaining eye was closed, it was no longer respectable to talk to it. Plus, it wasn't logical. His strange fancy to talk to the expired CleanerBot—to confess—had cost him everything. It had been a stupid decision. Ridiculously stupid.

He scanned his logs, wondering what to do next. Nova—it was time to tell her the truth. At this point, he had nothing to lose. He switched his internal comm on, then tapped the Ghostbusters pin.

"Nova, come in. It's Block. Can you talk?"

Silence.

Perhaps she was busy. He waited a minute. "Nova, come in. It's Block, I need to talk. It's important."

After twenty more seconds of waiting, there was a static burst preceding her voice. *Block, it's me.* Her voice faded and then rose, as if the signal were weak.

"I have terrible news. I've lost Wally. Cybel Venatrix has her, and I'm handcuffed in a room. I can't unlock myself. I can't protect Wally from here."

What? Okay, slow down. Let's figure this out. What happened?

"There's something I didn't tell you. I'm sorry."

She paused and the tone of her voice shifted. *What is it?*

"Wally's special. The reason that Mach X wants her—"

A sudden burst of banging and clattering sounded from the big tunnel. He paused. Footsteps?

Block?

"Sorry." The shaft that led into the salvage room was still empty. "I thought I heard something."

What's happening? Where's Wally?

"I don't know at this exact moment. I'm restrained and can't get free."

Nova paused, and there was background noise. Her voice muffled for a moment; it sounded like she was saying something but didn't want him to hear. *Why did the other robots lock you up? Why do they want Wally?*

"They think I did something wrong. That I lied to them, but I was only trying to protect Wally."

We'll come help you escape, destroy the other robots.

Destroy? Nova said it like it was matter of fact, but that's not what Block wanted at all.

Why does X want Wally? You were about to tell me.

Block processed scenarios, weighing whether telling

Nova the truth offered him any advantage. He was fifty-nine percent sure it did not.

"I don't understand why X wants her. I'm just a CleanerBot."

Then why did you say you had something to tell me?

"I needed your attention. What do I do? I'm stuck, and Cybel chased after Wally and commanded the other robots to find her. They could be hurting her. They don't know her like we do. They don't love her."

Nova fell silent.

"Nova? We have to protect her. She's our Wally. You agree, don't you?"

Of course. She wasn't sleeping lately. Block could tell from her strained voice.

"Where are you?"

We're in Tucson, scavenging supplies and recruiting help for staking out our next move.

"Mach X's forces are very close. We must protect Wally."

She didn't answer. Was she suspicious?

"What do we do?"

I'm just thinking. I'm not as fast as you. He knew that tone. Irritation.

As he waited for her to think, he processed 342 scenarios. In most of them, he was stuck to the scrapheap, unable to do anything.

Look for a weapon, anything around you. Something sharp you could use to break free of the metal. You're going to need to be able to protect yourself and take down other robots. What happened to the gun I gave you?

"But I'm just a CleanerBot. I don't use guns. There are SoldierBots here and even a few stronger robots. Also, there's a Mech. He's been nice to me, but when he finds out I lied, he won't be happy."

There must be something you can do. You have to figure out something for Wally's sake. The longer she's away from you, the more harm they can do.

He scanned the nearby scrap, spying shards of metal, rusty nails, and a few pieces of coils and wires. "There's nothing near me. No weapons or anything sharp, really. I'm stuck."

What about that virus you created? The one used on the drones. Could you use it on other robots?

"I'm a CleanerBot, unable to program sophisticated software and hack anything but drones."

He heard something loud on Nova's end. *Oh, crap. Look, I have to go. We're in the middle of negotiations. It's important we get more weapons. Figure something out.*

"But there's nothing I can do."

I'll be in touch soon. I believe in you. Figure it out. She said the last bit slowly. Firmly. Then there was static, and the signal died.

Block kicked his legs again, trying to break the metal restraints. Cybel had tied it strong because she was able to bend steel. He wasn't.

Could he clean his way out of this? He leaned forward and opened his back panel, extending suction tubes and hoses. They rose up from his back as if following a snake charmer. With the tubes, he reached above into the scrapheap and rotated his head so he could trace their path. All he could glimpse was more metal, pieces of damaged robots, and a few batteries that looked scorched. He stretched his longest vacuum hose, using it to upset rubble that lay out of view. A pile of metal and scrap bits rained down like a mini-landslide next to him.

He was lucky. Had he knocked it a few inches to the right, it would have buried him.

He withdrew his cleaning extensions, tucking them away. With his free arm, he rooted around the scrap that had rained down. The pile was three feet high, and he dug through it, scanning for anything valuable. Anything he could use as a weapon. He found a blade, though it looked like something that had been ripped off the arm of a SoldierBot. The blade was warped, its edge dull. It had probably been in a fire. He tossed it aside.

He discovered a black box device and studied it, not sure what it could do. A button on the side indicated it could be adjusted, but he had no idea what it actually did. He set it aside.

After more digging, he retrieved a screwdriver, hammer, and nails. Better than nothing. He grabbed the end of the hammer and swung at the iron rod, trying to knock it loose. The clanging of metal on metal was abrupt and echoed inside the chamber. He scanned around, alarmed that someone might have heard him. But the rhythmic pounding from the hall drowned out any loud noise. He pummeled the rod again, matching the rhythm this time.

Slam. Crash. Clang. With each blow, the hammer nudged the rod a fraction of an inch. After two hours of wailing on the rod, it had shifted only one inch and would give no farther. He laid the hammer down. He needed another plan.

Block's logic module spun and processed scenarios for another four hours. Nobody was coming for him. Low on fuel, he picked through the rubble and fed his stomach with bits of rubber and grease from the junky bits.

"Think," he said out loud, as if it would help. What

would Mr. Wallace do? His former hotel manager was smart, resourceful, and ever optimistic. He looked down at the dead CleanerBot. "I'll tell you what he wouldn't do. Mr. Wallace would never give up." Block picked up the hammer again and rammed it against the iron rod. It gave way half an inch this time. "You see?"

His gaze fell on the black device, and he picked up the rectangular box again. "Another thing about Mr. Wallace was his intense curiosity. He liked to figure out how things worked." Block nodded at the dead Cleaner-Bot. "I'm talking about my old boss, Mr. Wallace. I wish you could have seen The Drake. It was the most beautiful hotel, one of the finest in the world."

He held the device in his free hand; it rested in his palm. He shook it. It didn't seem to do anything. "Oh, well." He tossed it aside, and it bounced off the ground and vibrated loudly. A small screen on its side lit up. "Curious." He sent a ping, reaching out for information.

Code scanner active, it relayed into his feed.

"Code scanner?"

Do you want to scan your code?

He hesitated. "Yes."

CleanerBot X4J6. Manufacturing date February 2043. And then the device started pinging him a list of other stats: his charge level, microbial biofuel levels, and something else interesting: *This model is permeable to threats of many kinds. Defense rating 1.2 of 10. Ready to launch invasive code?*

Block searched his archives for the term invasive code. A rather obscure reference came back saying that a rebel militia group had created invasive code devices that could hack into and let them commandeer certain robot models.

If it was true, he didn't want to risk any invasive code in his system.

The device asked again: *Ready to launch invasive code into CleanerBot X4J6?*

"No," Block said. "Stop asking that."

A new message entered his feed. *Ready to scan next model.*

The unmistakable tremor of Oxford's footsteps shook the ground from somewhere in the connecting tunnel. He would enter the salvage room in moments. Block couldn't be discovered with the device—it wasn't his anyway, yet something stopped him from tossing it back into the junk piles.

Well, he couldn't be caught with it or Cybel would have more accusations. He grabbed for the black box, but it had slid just out of reach. The thing rested in the middle of the main path that wound around the salvage stacks. No way would Oxford miss it, even from his great height.

Block calculated the distance compared to the length of the hydraulic tubes in his cleaning extensions. Conceivably he could latch onto the device with a hose, but there was no time to be graceful!

Oxford's figure loomed in the tunnel's archway. Block stretched out his legs and kicked the device backward with his new heels—a lucky pass. The box skidded his way, and he scooped it up with his free hand, then tucked it in his thigh compartment.

Chapter 27
It's just something in her brain

Block's synthetic pathways hummed pleasantly when Oxford's enormous metal frame sauntered into the salvage room. No doubt the Mech would get him out of the restraints and clear up the misunderstanding with Cybel.

"Oxford, I'm over here." He waved his free hand as Oxford scanned the piles.

The Mech approached, knocking loose a pile that rained debris down around his feet, but the giant kept going.

"Cybel locked me up like this." Block expected Oxford to be angry at her, to come to his defense. But the robot halted and peered down at Block as if processing the situation. But what was there to decide?

"She locked me up and went after Wally. I'm very worried. Wally can't protect herself. There are many things that could fall on her. Robots could step on her or burn her accidentally." He paused, expecting Oxford to say something, anything, to back him up.

But the giant robot waited in silence, watching and looming over him.

Block shifted his bound feet and tried to sit straighter. Oxford's hydraulic joints hissed as he lowered his torso to the ground with a thud.

"You should've told me the truth." Oxford's voice was deep and gravelly. He punched both massive fists into the ground, creating tiny craters that rattled Block's frame from head to toe.

He knew upsetting Oxford was a risk. Well, he should've known. Every time lies were involved, something bad happened. Nova had lied about New Denver; that was bad—Block had gotten shot. Then Block had lied about the tunnel underneath the school; that was bad because now he'd ended up here, and Wally was in danger. And not telling the truth about Wally's implant had led to this.

"I am sorry." He meant it. "I should have told the truth, but I didn't want Wally to be hurt."

Oxford processed his confession and said nothing.

"Please, let me be with Wally. Cybel will do something to her, something awful. Something that might hurt her."

"The child is safe," Oxford's voice boomed.

"Can I be let loose and see her? I'm the only one she knows."

"It's too dangerous."

"What's too dangerous? Is Wally in trouble?"

"No, the girl is fine, but I can't let you free. Cybel suspects you'll try to escape with the child."

Block shook his foot restraints. "I can't even get out of the mess I'm in here. How do you think I could manage to escape?"

"I agree that you would try. It's obvious that your primary directive is to keep Wally safe at whatever cost. Cybel searched your bag and found a gun. What were you planning to do with it?"

"That wasn't mine! A human put it in my bag at Hemlock camp. I didn't find it until I was already on the road with Cybel." Block twisted against the restraints, trying to justify the weapon. This looked bad.

And Oxford was right—if Wally was in Block's arms, and there was a chance to be free of this mine, Cybel, and the coming war, he would flee in an instant.

A rusty patch showed where Oxford's hip hydraulic connected to his frame. He shifted his torso, resettling himself. "You disappointed me, Block."

Oh, no. Block hated to disappoint anyone, especially someone he liked.

"We took you in," Oxford continued. "I welcomed you as one of us, sheltered you here. And all the while, you were spying. Giving valuable information to Mach X."

"But that's not how it was, actually."

"Does the child have a neural implant that allows Mach X to observe?"

"Yes."

"Then how is that not spying?"

"Logically, yes. It is spying. But Wally didn't mean to do it. She can't help it. It's just something in her brain."

"If you'd told us the truth, we could have taken precautions. Perhaps we could have blindfolded her or kept her away from the others."

"I suppose that's true," Block said. "But Wally wouldn't have been happy blindfolded. She wouldn't have understood what was going on, and she would've cried. You don't know her like I do. I know about babies."

"You have a point. None of us know anything about children, and there are no NannyBots here. It's a fair point, but like I said, you must stay here for now."

"What is Cybel doing to Wally? Bring her in here with me, where she won't see what's happening out there. She can't give any information to X that way."

There was a loud hiss when Oxford rose and towered over him. Block calculated scenarios if he were to face Oxford as an adversary, but stopped after three because it was pointless—there was no chance for Block to win in that situation. "It's too late. The child must be kept with me and Cybel. Wally is valuable. Mach X wants her, presumably alive. We will use her if we have to."

"Use her? For what? She's just a child."

"Perhaps to bargain with. Perhaps as a security shield."

"Not you." Block yanked his wrist against the rod to which he was secured. His threat level indicator was rising. He wasn't in any immediate threat, but Wally was! "Cybel might harm her, but you, Oxford, you're different. You wouldn't risk Wally's life like that."

"I'm sorry Block. This is the way it must be." Oxford wheeled and marched away.

"Oxford, no." Block was not against begging. "Please, let me come with you. Keep my hands cuffed. I couldn't take Wally that way."

Oxford lurched forward another step, then paused.

"I won't be any trouble," Block said. "I promise."

"I trusted you before, and you betrayed me."

"Never again. I'm the only one who can protect Wally." He meant it. No more lies.

Oxford stood with his back to Block, making Block wonder what scenarios he was processing. Had he managed to convince Oxford? Being left alone here was the worst outcome. He had to get back to Wally.

A loud boom devastated the silence of the scavenger room. Dust and rubble from the mine's walls rained down.

Oxford faced Block. "They are here."

"All the more reason to let me care for Wally. I can protect her while you and Cybel defend the mine."

Oxford tilted his head. "You're a CleanerBot, so you're no threat to us." He lifted his metal arm and pointed one huge finger that was the size of Block's entire wrist. "If you try to escape, I'll be forced to hurt you." Oxford glanced at the dead CleanerBot, then back at Block. "Do you understand me?"

Block could not end up like the scorched and charred CleanerBot. For Wally's sake. "Yes, I understand."

Oxford lumbered over and snapped Block's steel restraints as if they were toothpicks. "Follow me."

Block rose, glanced once more at the expired CleanerBot—rest in peace—and hurried through the tunnel and into the robot hall.

Chaos abounded. The tremor from the outside explosions had affected the big room. A dusty haze floated in the air—particles from the walls, long dormant, had been disturbed. The robots were not so orderly anymore. They sidestepped rubble that had scattered on the ground. Oxford stomped through everything in his way, even knocking aside a FactoryBot who made the mistake of veering into the Mech's path.

"Sorry, sir," the bot said.

Oxford grunted in reply. The Mech headed straight

for Cybel. Block followed closely, having to duck and swerve a few times as Factory and SoldierBots raced around, scrambling for weapons and explosives.

They arrived at a long table near LB's workbench where Cybel stood, working on a huge tablet screen that was connected to others. She manipulated a hologram that floated above the modules. LB and Maxwell worked at the next table.

LB's head jerked when he saw Block. He sent a private ping. *I'm sorry. Cybel made us tell her about Wally's suit.*

I understand, Block replied.

Block scanned, searching for Wally. There was no sign of her. "Where is she?"

Oxford halted just before reaching Cybel. "Where is the child?"

"Down there." Cybel tilted her head sideways. She had locked Wally in place with the suit, and though the baby kicked her feet and wiggled her arms, she wasn't able to run. The suit held her in suspension, inches off the ground.

"We're under attack," Oxford's voice boomed and echoed in the hall. "Why aren't you out commanding our troops?"

Cybel paused the hologram. "For one thing, I was too busy dealing with the CleanerBot's treachery. I can't believe you ever trusted that thing."

"There's no time for this foolishness," Oxford said. "What's the plan for defense?"

"That's what I'm working on." She restarted the hologram, manipulating it to render a simulation of the outside battlegrounds. It appeared that Mach X's forces were amassed on the opposite side of the canyon and along the dusty road that led in.

"What about the mines we set up? Are they holding them off?"

"Thanks to the CleanerBot's treachery, they are disabling the mines by using their drones to disrupt them. Guess we have proof the child is able to send X messages."

Block stepped forward. "That's not true."

But Oxford interrupted. "Enough. Block, stay back. You've seen that the child is safe."

"I'm getting a ping." After a second's pause, Cybel said, "Our Bots are pushing away X's forces."

"They are? How?" Oxford asked.

"X's drones are recirculating and attacking their own troops. It was the virus from the CleanerBot."

LB chimed in. "Block's drone virus worked?"

"Heck, yeah!" Maxwell said.

"Silence," Cybel shouted. "We're not out of this yet."

Oxford shifted slightly in Block's direction. "Good job, Block."

Hearing such a compliment from Oxford was nice. Very nice.

Chapter 28
Old mining dust

Cybel studied the screens in the command unit that gave her a view of the canyon fighting outside. She and Oxford both twitched at the constant pings from their troops who relayed damage reports and attack patterns.

Unguarded, Block crept over to Wally and crouched down at eye level. She gazed at him, smiling and attempting to wave, though she couldn't bring her hands together in the restrictive, locked-down suit. No friendly clap like she normally gave Block upon spotting him.

"How are you?" Block asked in his lowest tone setting. He smoothed a fluttering strand of hair and checked the temperature of her cheek. Normal. No outward signs of abuse at Cybel's hands, and well, she was smiling.

"Block," she said.

"Hey. That's the first time you actually said my name."

She giggled. He swiveled his head to spy on Cybel and Oxford who were equally immersed in tracking the outside battle. He found it illogical that his drone virus had worked so well. He hadn't put much time into it at all, and his efforts were actually helping Oxford and Cybel. He pressed the button on Wally's suit collar to release her from suspension and scooped her up. Expecting to get yelled at and have her taken away at any moment, he rotated his head to face their angry wrath, but nothing. They hadn't noticed him.

Block excelled at being invisible. He could try to walk out of the room, through the tunnel, and into the desert, but they'd certainly catch his movement and detain him. Nevertheless, he would not mess up this time. At Hemlock, he'd misjudged. He should have fled through the tunnel with Wally when he'd had the chance, but instead he hung back for Nova and the others. He would not make that mistake again. Wally's safety was the only thing that mattered.

Cybel jerked her head suddenly. "What are you doing?"

"Block, no," Oxford's voice echoed along the cavernous walls. "Wally must stay here. You're free to go, but she stays."

Cybel said, "Why don't you head outside, Cleaner-Bot? Let's see how you fare."

"Show respect," Oxford said.

Block stood his ground even though he wasn't used to talking back to bigger, powerful robots. "I'm not going anywhere, and I will *not* be away from Wally. You can keep us wherever you want, hide us if you must, but I'm not leaving her side."

Something on Cybel's screen was going berserk. "What's happening now?" Oxford asked.

"I'm trying to process." She was engrossed in the holographic display screens. "Something's changed."

At the next table, LB and Maxwell hovered over a

complicated assembly, a cylindrical device made from an eggplant purple metal. It was long and wide and portable.

Block edged toward them, trying to stay low on Oxford's and Cybel's radars. "What are you doing?"

"Assembling a rocket launcher," LB said. "You know, what all LaundryBots do after they retire from the hospitality industry."

Block backed away from the table. Maxwell was a good engineer, but his flashing threat indicator told him Wally shouldn't be close to the volatile weapon.

Maxwell was doing most of the work while LB watched and passed along tools. LB raised his arms halfway, his version of a shrug. "Never pictured myself here, doing this in the middle of a war, but times are strange."

Block placed his arms around Wally, hugging her while she babbled. "I suppose I never predicted a place like this either."

A boom resonated from somewhere in the hills above. More dust rained down from the mine's ceiling, coating the air in a hazy film. Block extended his vacuum tube, applied the highest air filter setting, and tried to clean the space in which Wally was breathing. Old mining dust was probably no good for a child to inhale.

"Will the walls hold?" Block asked.

"Judging by my calculations, not for long." Maxwell didn't look up from his delicate operation.

Block's threat level indicator starting pinging—trying to register a full alert. That settled it. He had to find a way out of the mine, and soon. He couldn't risk a cave-in where Wally could be killed. One scenario bubbled up from his processor—one where they became trapped inside the mine without food and water. Devasting.

"There's time, though," Maxwell said. "We've been

reinforcing the walls. They were originally built pretty solid, but over time there's been decay. Should last anywhere from a few hours to several weeks."

"What? That's a wide range," Block said.

"Yeah, buddy," LB said. "Can you narrow it down a little?"

"No, I really can't." Maxwell began soldering.

"I knew it was too easy!" Cybel slammed both metal fists against the tabletop, bending the thick steel legs under her fury and nearly knocking the computer station over.

"Report," Oxford said. He was too tall to see the screens.

"The drones were a ruse. X's forces are pushing in, stronger than before."

"What do you mean a ruse?"

"They tricked us," Cybel said. "Either they figured it out quickly, or they wanted us to think we were winning. I'm not entirely certain. We're not winning. We're barely holding them off."

Oxford lowered his head. "We tried our best. It's time for you and I to join the fight."

Cybel squeezed her fists. "There must be something else to bring them down."

"We keep the girl here, safe. That's all we can do now. We have the one thing X wants." Oxford glanced at Block.

"Yes," Cybel said. "Protect our bargaining chip. I'll order two SoldierBots to guard them."

"No." Oxford shifted on his elephant-sized legs. "We need every fighting bot outside."

"Well, what do you propose? We can't have the CleanerBot walk off with our prize."

"She's a human being, not a prize or some chip you can negotiate with," Oxford said. "I'll stay and hold off any machines who try to enter this tunnel. I'll protect Wally and Block."

"But you could fight for us out there. Help us win," Cybel said. "We need your strength."

"I wish there were ten more of me. But there's just me, and I'll need to make a last stand in here. Guard the mine, guard the child."

Block didn't like where this conversation was going. He was glad they wanted to protect Wally, but could Oxford really fight off Mach X's forces if they invaded the mine? He was only one machine. A combat war Mech was strong, but could he fight off an army?

"Nothing about protecting us," LB muttered to Maxwell.

Cybel jerked her head, irritated. "Are you about done with that launcher? You've been assembling it for ages."

"Yes, Commander. Nearly done," Maxwell said, going back to work.

"Go," Oxford told Cybel. "They need you out there. You're our best commander."

"Finally, you admit my superiority." She raised her arm in a fist. "Be safe."

Oxford tapped his hand to hers. "Stay strong, friend."

Cybel spun to leave, then halted. "Wait. Give me that rocket launcher." She approached their table.

Block gave her plenty of space to pass as Maxwell's hands flew about and morphed into a blur as he finished the launcher. "Done, Commander."

She held it, admiring the work, then rested the base against her shoulder. With a last glance at Block and Wally, she strode into the tunnel.

A tremor shook the great room, then another series of smaller explosions sounded from the earth above. Block cradled Wally, shielding her head with his arms. He was nowhere near as much protection as Oxford, but it was something. If only he could win Oxford to his side.

A logic warning in Block's core advised him not to speak up. It was his timidity programming—hardcoded to prevent him from saying inappropriate things to hotel guests. Unfortunately, it now worked against him. He fought it, knowing he must say something. "Oxford, what are we doing here? Waiting for SoldierBots to flood the tunnel? This is ludicrous. We must escape."

Oxford lowered his torso to the ground and rested. "We stay here. This is where we make a last stand."

"A last stand for what?" Block had hoped LB and Maxwell might chime in, but they lingered near their workbench, stone silent.

Block ignored his flashing timidity warning again. "To be destroyed when they take over the mine? Is that what you want? For them to take Wally and leave us lying in mangled heaps of warped metal?" Block didn't want to end up looking like the dead CleanerBot. Who would shut his eyelids?

It seemed that no one cared except him. He needed to fight for what he believed in.

"I know it's a strange situation," Block continued. "Mach X implanted something in Wally's head. But I'm telling you, she's a good girl. She loves people, robots, and animals. She smiles. Laughs."

"Cries," LB said.

"Yes, she's human. She cries, sleeps, eats, excretes—like all humans. But she's more than that. She's special.

She is capable of great things if we give her the chance. She's very intelligent for her age."

"Humans aren't that intelligent. Not like us," Oxford said.

"But she *is* like us. In a way," Block said. "She's human but has intelligence from Mach X too. The other day, she solved a complicated puzzle—a Rubik's Cube! It should have been impossible for her young age, but she did it. Many adults have never solved that puzzle."

"What are you trying to convince me of?" Oxford asked.

"Wally is worth fighting for. We can't let Mach X capture her. It will corrupt her, turn her against us. We have no idea what X is planning to do with her."

"That's not my problem."

"But it is—it's all of our problems. Before, you said you believed in a more peaceful world. You've convinced your troops of your mission—to stop X's plans for human annihilation."

"So?"

"What if Wally's a piece of the puzzle? What if she's the key to solving the problem? She's part human, part machine. She can be an envoy between humans and AI."

"Whoa, that's deep," Maxwell said.

"You paint a pretty picture, but there is no time for lofty ambitions." Oxford rose to his full height. "X's forces will enter the mine. Prepare yourself."

Chapter 29
Oxford is broken

Oxford paced the wide room. His head jerked to the right, catching a comm from outside. "We don't have much time. Our troops are being overpowered."

Block tightened his hold around Wally's tiny frame. Even with an armored suit, he wasn't sure it would be enough.

Something vibrated inside Block's thigh compartment. Odd. Ignoring it, he looked around for the backpack with Wally's food and water. He found it and swung it onto his back.

"You make an odd-looking CleanerBot," Maxwell said.

LB said, "Loaded in the front and the back. We're stuck in here. You might as well try to make yourself comfortable. Oxford will protect us."

"Against an army?"

"My scenarios don't look good either," LB said. "But there's not much we can control."

Whatever was in Block's leg compartment twitched and buzzed. It rattled his thigh and was so annoying, he opened it, grabbing for the source of the disturbance. It was the device he'd found in the scrap room. A message flashed in his feed: *Connect with model DZG-LD?*

Block didn't recognize the model name. It was as if the device was trying to connect with a nearby robot, but it wasn't a LaundryBot's brand. He saw a serial number that started with G on Maxwell—all FactoryBots started with G. That only left Oxford. Would the device somehow be able to hack into a Mech? That was entirely ridiculous. No way such a small device would let him gain access to a powerful robot. He started to stow the device back into his compartment, but it buzzed in his hand so suddenly he nearly dropped it.

Connect with model DZG-LD? Waiting...

He looked at Oxford. The mechanical giant rested one arm against the wall. To them he was silent, but he was probably engaged in comms, trying to direct the forces outside. Oxford was there to protect them, and it was inevitable that the SoldierBots would invade. Block ran scenarios: as strong as Oxford was, as much as he fought to defend them, the Mech was destroyed in 87.9 percent of the scenarios. Even worse, 99.25 percent of the time, Wally was taken, and Block was destroyed.

That was unacceptable.

He studied the device. This was the unknown variable in his scenario processing, and even if it gave him a one percent chance, wasn't that worth the risk?

He pressed the button on the device's side, but nothing happened. Well, that was a lot of processing power for nothing. He tossed it back in his leg and shut the panel.

He bounced, jiggling Wally. Should he change her? Maybe it didn't matter, but if she was abducted, he didn't want her to be uncomfortable—especially around robots who didn't know how to care for her. He shuffled over to an empty table and lifted a diaper from the backpack, set Wally down, and changed her.

LB and Maxwell watched. "How often do you have to do that?" LB asked.

"Seven or eight times a day."

"Oh. It doesn't look too difficult," Maxwell said.

Block finished and put Wally back in the chest carrier, but as he tried to fold the armored suit and place it in the backpack, he struggled. The fabric didn't bend like regular clothes.

"She should wear it," Maxwell said. "It conforms to her body."

"Can it fit while she's in the carrier?" Block asked.

"Like a second skin."

Wally grinned as she touched the suit and wiggled into it as Block slid the top and bottom back on. Maxwell was right—the shiny metal morphed and clung to her like a protective barrier. Block worried that the alloy would chafe her skin while she rode in the carrier, but she showed no distress when he settled her in her usual seat against his torso.

He spun toward the others, but something seemed wrong.

Oxford stood near the entrance to the mine shaft. His head was lowered, and his arms hung at his sides. Somehow, he looked like a lifeless puppet waiting for someone to pull his strings.

Block approached. "Oxford? Are you okay?"

No answer. That was unusual.

The device buzzed in his leg. It pinged him: *DZG-LD awaiting instructions. Speak your commands.*

What was happening? "Oxford? Please say something."

Oxford stirred, and a garbled noise came from his voice box, but his head still hung low, staring at the ground. It was as if he'd been turned off. This was not good.

More explosions pounded the rock layers above. The walls shook.

"We need to get out of here," Block shouted over his shoulder to LB and Maxwell. "Oxford is broken."

They rushed over. "What do you mean, broken?"

"I don't know," Block said. "He won't move."

"What's that in your hand?" Maxwell asked.

"Something I found in the scrap room." Block held it out.

"A hack box? Do you know what that is?"

"Not really."

"It's incredibly rare. Oxford and Cybel ordered us to destroy any we found. We must have missed this one."

"Well, what does it do?"

"It lets you hack into a robot and control it. Some genius human rebel created them and had a batch of like, five hundred of them. Rumor has it, Mach X tracked this guy down and gave him a slow and painful death. But the devices had gotten out already." Maxwell looked at Oxford. "Did you use this on him?"

Block gazed up at the towering giant, then glanced at the device. "Yes, I suppose I did. It was an accident."

"If this works, you now control Oxford. I heard these things last for several hours. It's not just a switch you can turn on and off. You have to control him, or he just stands there."

"But I don't know how or what to do with him." Block

shifted, bouncing Wally who was beginning to fuss. The walls shook again, throwing up dust clouds. "What do I do?"

LB and Maxwell looked at each other, probably messaging each other inaudibly. "I suppose you could bust us out of here," LB said. "You control a badass Mech."

Block didn't know the first thing about Mechs other than that they were gigantic, made of steel, and something he should stay far, far away from.

"I made a mistake." Block backed away from Oxford and looked at the device. "There must be a way to shut this off, reverse it. Oxford will be furious."

"Once you hack a robot, you have control for hours," Maxwell said. "That's the way it was designed."

"But it's a misunderstanding," Block insisted. "Here, one of you take the device." He thrust his hand out.

Maxwell raised his hands. "Not me. I'm not controlling Oxford."

Block looked at LB. "Will you help me?"

He shrugged. "You know Oxford better than me. I think you should handle him. You're a lot smarter than me."

But that wasn't true. Block was just a CleanerBot. Definitely not smarter than any of the others.

At the far end of the tunnel, there was a clattering, followed quickly by loud gunfire. A deep burst sounded, and large flames lit the walls.

"They're trying to protect the tunnel," Maxwell said. "The SoldierBots could be coming through here any minute."

LB rattled as a tremor shook the walls. "Block, you'd better try something, or we're toast."

Why were they leaving it up to him? He looked at the device. "Do I tap on it?"

Maxwell craned his head, scanned it. "Try just talking at it."

"And say what?"

"Just make something up," LB said. "Use it like you were talking to Oxford."

"Really? That would work?"

"Try it out," LB said. "You've got this, Block. I believe in you."

Block appreciated the vote of confidence, but he didn't have much for himself. They were running out of time, so he had to try something. He felt silly talking into the device, but this wasn't the place to worry about appearances.

"Oxford, wake up," he spoke at the device.

Nothing happened for a second, and then slowly Oxford's leg hydraulics hissed. A whirring sound rose as Oxford bent his knees, moved his arms, and twisted his torso. He peered down at Block.

"Ready for your command." The words came out of Oxford's voice module, but it didn't sound like him. The timbre was flat and lacked his usual friendliness.

"Oxford?" Block asked.

"I am DZG-LD. Ready for your command."

Block looked at Maxwell and LB. "Where is Oxford?"

Maxwell said, "The hack box woke up some other part of him. Probably somewhere in his core—it's a shell of Oxford, but it's the one that will obey."

"Now what?"

"Tell him what to do," LB said. "Go into the tunnel, clear a path, we follow. Then Oxford shoots and destroys everything in his path. Seems pretty simple to me."

"If we could get out of the tunnel," Block said, "I know someone who will help us."

"You have a contact on the outside?" LB asked.

"Yes. She's a friend. I've known her for a while. Well, a few months. She'll help us."

"Good, I like meeting new Bots, especially of the female variety," LB said. "What's her model?"

Block didn't want to break the news that his friend was human. He didn't know what Maxwell and LB would think. "She's military grade."

"SoldierBot?"

"Sort of. An early model. We're losing time. We must make our move."

LB said, "We'll follow and help you."

Block stared up at Oxford. "I'm sorry about this. I didn't mean to hack you. It was kind of an accident, but I need your help to get us out of here."

He felt Maxwell's heavy hand on his shoulder. "You know he can't understand that, right?"

Block nodded. He needed to say it anyway. "Walk into the tunnel and arm your weapons. Prepare for battle." Block stepped back. "Does that sound right?"

"Crank my joints, I think it's working," Maxwell said.

Oxford lowered his arms and the ends of both fists rotated, humming as they morphed into gatling guns. From his back, a panel opened, and a missile cannon appeared, rose, and rested on his right shoulder.

"Wow," LB said. "This is intense."

Maxwell said quietly, "Tell him to ready his shields."

Shields? Block had no idea how these things worked. He'd never seen a Mech in action.

"His shield won't deflect everything," Maxwell

explained, "but it should be enough to get us out of harm's way and protect us."

"Ready your shield," Block commanded.

A hazy blue light, nearly invisible, illuminated the front of Oxford's body, surrounding him in what looked like a foggy halo.

"Excellent," Maxwell said.

"Are you both ready?" Block asked.

They nodded.

What they were about to attempt—a LaundryBot, a FactoryBot, an armored human baby, and a CleanerBot controlling a combat Mech—was lunacy.

Block knew the odds of escaping the mineshaft were not good, but there was no other choice.

Move or die.

Chapter 30
Fight or whatever

Block gripped the device and spoke. "Enter the tunnel. Three of us are behind you." He felt he owed Oxford an explanation of what was about to happen. "You will lead us out of the tunnel and fight against the enemy attackers. You must protect us."

Oxford buzzed, his hydraulics hissing. "Confirmed. I will eliminate enemy attackers and protect you."

"Not just me. I'm Block. This is Wally—she's important and cannot get hurt. And this is LB and Maxwell. You have to keep all of us safe, okay?"

"Confirmed," Oxford's deep voice boomed.

"Okay, now that's settled. Proceed." He wished he'd said it with more confidence. He should have asked Nigel to adjust his timidity setting. Or maybe Maxwell could have, but they were out of time.

"Proceed," Oxford repeated and stomped forward. His mechanical stride was the length of two CleanerBots stretched out head to toe.

The three smaller robots stepped in line behind Oxford. Block jogged to keep up, cradling Wally to keep her from jostling. He glanced back at LB and Maxwell following closely.

"LB, are you going to be able to walk out in the desert?" Like Block's own model, LaundryBots weren't meant for all-terrain travel.

"Yeah, I'll be fine. Maxwell outfitted me with new feet too, in case I had to go outside or fight or whatever."

"That's good." Block circled his attention back to Oxford. The tunnel was empty of other robots, and they soon reached the barrier where the elevator was, the spot where Ahtron had first dropped him and Wally off. The armored SUV was gone, presumably out in the battle with Cybel.

Oxford halted and waited for commands.

"Will the elevator hold Oxford?" Block asked.

"Yeah, but only him," Maxwell said. "We'll have to ride up after him."

"Oxford, I mean, DZG-LD, ride the elevator up to the higher level."

Oxford did as told, then lowered it back down, allowing Block and the others to step on and ascend. The elevator made it halfway when a massive explosion rocked the tunnel. There was no barrier on the flatbed elevator, and Block staggered and fell to his knees, clutching Wally who wailed. LB tumbled sideways and caught himself before the edge. Maxwell stumbled but righted himself. An after-tremor shook the elevator bed, so Block tightened one arm around Wally. LB started rolling, out of control. Block reached, caught his hand. Maxwell teetered and fell backward off the edge. A clatter rang out as he struck the ground.

"Maxwell!" LB cried out, but the elevator bed was still shaking. A loud twisting and twanging came from nearby—the cables suspending the elevator had been damaged. Block processed scenarios if they fell. Wally's armor might protect her, but Block and LB would surely be damaged. Worse, they would all be trapped down below.

LB crawled to the edge, peering down. "Maxwell, can you hear me? Are you okay?"

Maxwell answered faintly from below. "I'll make it. I have some damage, but it can be repaired."

"We're going to come down and get you," LB said.

"No," Maxwell shouted, louder this time. "Tell Oxford to reach down and lift you off the elevator. The cables are about to snap. Hurry. It won't hold for long."

LB shook his head. "We're not leaving you down there."

"You have to. I'm staying here. There's no other choice. No other way up, and that elevator is about to break. Save yourselves."

LB looked at Block. "Get us off here."

Block looked for the device. It had been in his hand, but the tremors must have knocked it from him. He scanned around. "Where is it?"

Then he spotted the square rectangular device by the edge where it had slid and nearly fallen. He grasped it. Over Wally's cries he said, "DZG-LD, reach down and get us off of this elevator."

Oxford glanced over the edge, then disappeared. Block's circuits raced. Was it possible he would disobey? Maybe the device didn't work as well as Maxwell thought it would.

Block stared up, waiting, and watched as Oxford's head reappeared, followed by one of his massive arms. He reached down, but it wasn't far enough to grab them. Just three feet short. Oxford grunted. Something buzzed, and with his other arm, he tossed down a thick cable. "Grab onto this. I will pull you up."

"You first," LB said.

Block tugged the line, uncertain how safe this was while holding Wally. But then the elevator trembled, and the suspension cable twanged under their weight. Block gave the device to Wally. Her red, tear-stained eyes widened in surprise. "Block?" She let out one more sob, then fixated on the device.

Block grabbed onto the cables with both hands. "I'm on. Pull!" he shouted.

Oxford began to hoist Block and Wally up, inches at a time. Block began calculating tensile strength, the speed of their ascent, and whether the elevator would fall before LB made it up.

They'd already lost Maxwell. LB had offered to help rescue him, but Maxwell had refused, sacrificing himself for their safety. It was a noble thing. What's more, LB hadn't argued. He'd accepted the decision and moved on. Block admired that. He wished he could make decisions as easily as LB had. All of his waffling had costed him dearly—he could have escaped with Wally at Hemlock. They would be free of all this mess.

Oxford hoisted them all the way until they reached the top. Then he lurched backward and raised the chain, lifting their bodies up, and bringing them toward him until Block's heels rested on firm ground. They were safe.

"Now lift up LB," Block said. Oxford obeyed, and he realized he didn't actually need to speak directly into the black box that controlled it.

After another two minutes, LB had reached safety too.

"We made it," Block said. "Let's get going." On this higher level, gunfire echoed against the tunnel walls.

Oxford stomped forward, but LB hesitated. "You go on," he said.

"Wait, what?" Block asked. Oxford halted, waiting for commands.

"I'm going to stick around and see if I can help Maxwell."

"But the SoldierBots will surely invade the mine. Maxwell is already damaged, and you both might be destroyed."

"I know." LB shrugged in his way. "It's a death wish, but Maxwell's my friend, and I don't want to leave him twisted and broken down there. I'm going to find a way to get down and help him. Then he and I are going to booby trap the hell out of this mine. We'll take down as many of those Mach X creeps as possible."

"Are you sure about this? I'll miss you."

"I'm positive. I'll miss you too. You're a good robot, Block. Look at all you've accomplished."

"What? Me?"

"You've made human friends, you've kept a baby safe —an incredibly important baby. And now you've helped me and Maxwell. You control a Mech. Where will it end with you? You're incredible."

Block wasn't sure why LB was saying all this. He couldn't blush like Wally, but his neural circuit pathways warmed up. "Thank you, LB. Please stay safe."

"I will." LB lifted one of his hooked hands and patted Block's shoulder. "You be safe out there. Take care of this girl. Use your badass Mech."

Block walked away with Oxford leading. His feed noted the elevation change and the rise in temperature, but it barely registered. His core processing was entirely consumed by the fact that they were about to run into a small war waging outside.

And he was just a CleanerBot.

A CleanerBot with a baby to protect.

Chapter 31
Metal tendrils

"Nova, come in," Block said. "We're leaving the mine."

He heard her voice after a few seconds. *I read you. Sending you our geo-coordinates. We're fifty-five klicks from you.*

Block wasn't entirely sure what a klick was, but he didn't have time to ask now. "Can't talk. Need to focus on getting us out of the line of fire. Will contact you once we're free and clear. Over."

Holy —

He tapped the comm off. He'd had enough of good-byes for today. Oxford's pumping gigantic legs protected them in front. The ground trembled beneath Oxford's heels, his arm firepower was switched on, and his shoulder cannon was poised.

"Shields up," Block said. A thin, glowing blue haze surrounded Oxford's body in the near-pitch blackness of the mine shaft. "Remember, you must protect us."

Oxford—actually, the automaton now inhabiting Oxford—halted and looked at Block and Wally. In her carrier, Wally wiggled closer against Block's chest and buried her face.

"I will protect you," Oxford said. Then something odd happened. He shifted forward and kneeled. "Climb onto my back. It's safer there. You'll be shielded."

"On your back?" Block wasn't sure about the proposition. His scenarios hadn't accounted for this. He hated when new scenarios came at him from nowhere.

"Get on," Oxford said. They'd nearly reached the entrance. Several FactoryBots had formed a line to guard the mine's entrance. Heavy gunfire pounded the mouth of the cave from outside. There was no avoiding the dangerous battle.

If Wally got hit...

He looked down at her and pressed the button near her collar that engaged the shield in her suit armor. The helmet rose up and covered her face and head. Maxwell had said it was bullet resistant, and he hoped that was true. He needed to scale Oxford's steep back panel, so he stepped onto a steel barrel, then thrust his foot onto Oxford's elbow joint to boost himself up. Grasping, he found Oxford's neck and grabbed hold.

Block hung from Oxford's back, his entire body exposed, but quick scenario processing revealed that he would be safer attached to Oxford then running behind him under heavy gunfire.

Oxford asked, "Are you secure?"

Block wiggled his body to get a solid purchase on the giant robot's back. He glanced down at Wally who seemed okay even though she was sandwiched between him and Oxford's back. Her armor should buffer her against shocks and jolts. She seemed brave, not even crying as she stared out from behind her visor.

"We're secure."

Oxford rose to full height and stormed through the tunnel, easily closing the thirty feet to the mine entrance.

"Make way!" Oxford's voice boomed at the Factory-Bots who still managed to guard the entrance. Two that were badly damaged had been dragged over to the side. On one inert bot, smoke coiled from its CPU. Three remaining FactoryBots had formed a barricade and hunkered behind a four-foot-high concrete wall. As Oxford neared, they scurried out of his path. Oxford moved forward, hopping the barrier as if it was a twig on a foot path. He passed through the mine's entrance, and they emerged into the canyon valley. Steep hills surrounded them on all sides, made visible through night vision. On higher ground, Mach X's troops fired. Bursts of bright light flared in Block's input screen as bullets shredded the dry desert ground around Oxford, but his shield deflected them, scattering shrapnel. Oxford raised his arms and triggered a hailstorm of automatic rounds. He pointed his left arm straight ahead at the hill facing the mine entrance. A quick pivot—Block was surprised at how the enormous Mech could move so swiftly—and he stretched his other arm at the cliffs above the mine where another group of enemy forces had amassed.

The firepower burst from his arms and rocked Oxford's whole body, rattling Block and Wally. Good thing he'd activated her armor. The enemy robots on the canyon tops seemed to retreat now that they faced a furious Mech.

Block spotted Cybel and Ahtron. The SUV's armor was fully raised, and Cybel and a friendly SoldierBot hunkered behind, using the vehicle as a shield. Two spider-shaped WarBots had locked in on their position.

Along with two enemy SoldierBots, they were closing in, unleashing heavy firepower. Cybel and her crew were trapped.

Block shouted, "Help Cybel!"

Oxford, still firing, swiveled his head and sprinted toward Ahtron and Cybel. The SpiderBots were powerful, but they were no match for a Mech. At twelve feet, Oxford was twice their height. Oxford skidded to a stop, lifted one giant leg in the air, and stomped down on one SpiderBot. It hissed and a violent scream ejected from its voicebox. Smoke poured out of its mangled, dented body. Then Oxford set his sights on the second one, but it had seen what happened to its companion. It backed up, spraying gunfire across Oxford's front, but the bullets were deflected. It whipped one of its metal tendrils and gripped Oxford's right ankle. Another long coil looped around Oxford's left leg, this one higher. The SpiderBot had a shield of its own that deflected Oxford's firepower. Oxford lunged forward and stumbled, caught by the tendrils around his legs and feet. Lowering his right arm, Oxford swung his fist, knocking two SoldierBots away like they were bowling pins.

Block held on tight. It was all he could do. Cybel raced out from behind the barricade, gripping an axe and chopping away at the SpiderBot's tendrils. Oxford tripped and landed on his knees with a deafening crash, but it got him close to the bot. One massive punch, and his metal fist struck the SpiderBot's oval center. A high-pitched hiss emerged as hydraulic fluid leaked onto the desert soil. The tendrils fell away, and Oxford stood again.

Cybel shouted, "What happened? I've been trying to ping you forever."

But hacked Oxford just stared at her.

"What's wrong with you?" She kicked his leg.

"I am DZG-LD. Awaiting orders."

"Go northeast. Get us away from the fighting," Block said.

Cybel jerked her head at Block. "What are you talking about?" She regarded Oxford—or this shell of who she thought Oxford was. "What did you do to him?"

"Get us away from the fighting," Oxford repeated, and began to sprint.

"Come back here!" Cybel shouted. "Help end this! Don't leave us."

Block heard her pleas and felt an odd twitch about leaving them on their own to face Mach X, but he was done with old mistakes.

His body rattled and shook against Oxford's back as his giant steel legs pounded the earth below. Block twisted his head to look back as they cleared the canyon. No one followed.

Oxford ran along the dirt road they'd traveled in on. Fifty feet ahead, a group of SoldierBots and an armored SUV were stationed—a checkpoint or barricade. As Oxford surged toward it, they readied their weapons and fired, but Oxford plowed through them, swiping the SoldierBots down into the canyon like dominoes falling from a table. The SUV thrust up its armor and revved its engines. A hood cannon just like Ahtron's started to emerge, but Oxford was fast to react. He spun and lifted the car up by its frame and tossed it over the edge of the road.

Screeching metal and an explosion sounded. Flames erupted on the hillside below, blinding Block's night vision stream, but Oxford didn't hesitate. Wally's eyes were wide as she watched all of this happening from behind her visor. No doubt Mach X saw. Good. Maybe that would mean the supercomputer would think twice about tracking them now that he had Oxford.

Oxford sprinted down the dusty road, and Block surveyed the road ahead and behind. Nobody seemed to have followed. No drones tracked them from overhead. Or, if they did, he failed to detect them.

Block figured it was safe to contact Nova. He tapped the Ghostbusters pin and switched on his feed.

"Nova, come in."

I'm here. What happened? Are you okay?

"Wally and I are good. We're safe at the moment."

Where are you?

"We're heading toward you on the road leading out of the canyon."

How did you get past all those troops?

"You'll see when I get there."

What? Do you have some kind of new tech?

"Promise me that no harm will come to us."

What are you talking about? She sighed on her end. *Of course not. We're here to rescue you.*

"I have a friend with me, and I know that Shane's troops are scared of AI. I don't want them to hurt my friend."

Block, we're going to help you. We won't hurt one of your robot friends.

"You swear?"

I swear it.

"Thank you," Block said. "At this speed, we should get to you in fifty-nine minutes. How will we know where you are?"

"It's an Old West town. Like from the movies. You can't miss it."

Block had watched a Western once with Mr. Wallace. It had been called *Three Amigos*. Mr. Wallace had laughed and laughed throughout the film. Block mimicked his laughter, though he didn't understand all of the jokes.

He was interested to see a real Western town. Oxford reached the highway and raced along the cracked, dry asphalt. Wildflowers bloomed along the side of the road in uneven patches, but Block couldn't discern the color in the early dark hours. Block rotated his head to check the highway behind them. Far off, on the tiny road, heat trails swirled in the sky where the fighting waged on. Could someone be following them? He wasn't sure.

Best to keep moving.

Part Three
Survivors

Chapter 32
Grand Palace Hotel Saloon

"Slow down." Block's GPS told him they were close to where Nova had said she'd be, on the outskirts of Tucson in an abandoned Old West town. Block had made her promise not to hurt Oxford, but would she keep her word?

The sun teased the dry desert as it rose, illuminating jagged brown mountains to the north and west. After veering off the highway and trekking through scraggly desert brush, they found themselves on a dirt road. Four black birds circled above. Block's peripheral memory matched them to his archives—turkey vultures. The creatures typically fed on carrion and were much larger than Chicago pigeons.

"Walk slowly." Oxford still obeyed Block's voice commands. Wally gripped the device in her tiny hands. Perhaps she knew, somehow, how important it was. Given long enough, she would probably figure out how it worked like she did the Rubik's Cube.

He suspected she was far more intelligent than any

child her age was supposed to be. But how much of that was her, and how much was Mach X?

Oxford slowed to a normal pace, and Block considered telling him to tread more quietly, but it would be hopeless. A Mech couldn't help how much he weighed. His immense strength had gotten them clear of the fighting zone, and for that Block was grateful.

A cluster of buildings stood apart from the surrounding sparse trees and bushes. Two rotting pillars of logs supported a rusty chain from which a beaten sign hung: Old Tucson. It had been crossed out many times over and marred with spray paint.

Dirt lined the road that stretched between two main rows of structures with dilapidated wooden and stucco facades. Among them was a two-story building made of wood with long windows in front and a balcony on the second tier that looked fake. A sun-faded wooden sign hung: *Grand Palace Hotel Saloon.* Judging by the neglected shingles, Block didn't see anything grand about it.

A few other rickety buildings nearby added to the town's emptiness. The wooden shutters that still clung to the old architecture wanted to shrivel up. Paint peeled from every surface, and windows had been boarded up. It didn't look exactly like the *Three Amigos* movie, but this had to be what Nova described as the Old West.

A strange bird called out from nearby—a shrill, hooting sound. Then another hoot came from the opposite side of the town's Main Street, this one obviously from a human.

"Block." Nova stepped out of the saloon doors, clutching her rifle, but not aiming it. She wore camouflage pants, black boots, a dark T-shirt, and a navy blue bandanna wrapped around her head, tamping down her wild curls.

Block told Oxford, "Let us down now." The towering robot obeyed and lowered so Block could step off. As soon as he stood on solid ground, he checked on Wally.

"Are you okay?" He touched the button on her collar to lower the visor.

She grinned. "Bwock."

He patted her suit chest. "Good girl."

Nova sprinted over and threw her arms around Block and Wally. "Oh my God, I can't believe it. Are you both all right?" But all the while, she eyed Oxford. "This is the friend you were talking about?"

"Yes, this is Oxford. He's the reason we got clear of the SoldierBots."

"I see." She touched the side of her head and spoke into a comm. "The Mech is with us, hold your fire."

"Hold your fire?" Block asked. "Why would you aim guns at us?"

"Because we saw a damn Mech approaching. What did you expect us to do? I couldn't tell you were on its back until you got close."

"You would have fired at us?"

She scowled. "Come on. Let's get you inside and get Wally cleaned up. Check for injuries. Helen is here and she's dying to see Wally."

"What about Oxford?"

The big Mech lingered ten feet away, waiting on Block's commands.

"Can you disable it? We can't just leave it around here."

Two men emerged from inside a smaller building,

pointing their rifles at Oxford. Another two armed troops came out of the saloon's swinging doors.

"Oxford's my friend," Block said. "You promised you wouldn't hurt my friend."

Nova shouldered her rifle and thrust her hands on her hips. "I know I said that, but I didn't know you were talking about a *Mech*. I expected another CleanerBot like you or a FactoryBot. You didn't say you were bringing a walking tank."

Nova's soldiers—two men and two women—surrounded Oxford. He stepped back, lifted his arms, and rotated the gun barrels inside his arms, ready to defend himself.

Nova's face blanched.

Block called out, "Do not fire. I repeat, do not fire."

Oxford lowered his cannon arms and looked at Block. "Awaiting instructions."

One of Nova's men trained his rifle on Block, then Oxford, moving back and forth as if confused about who was in control.

Block spied a shady spot next to a battered building that looked like a barn but was meant for horses. "Go sit against the stable."

Oxford obeyed, and Block looked at Nova. "Are you satisfied now?"

"Fletcher, we have this under control," she said to the man who couldn't decide his target.

But he aimed at Block. "Under control?" Fletcher's voice was low and gravelly. "There's a huge Mech here. At any moment it could go berserk and kill us all."

"This is Block, the one I was telling you about. He won't let that happen. The Mech is his friend. He controls it."

"How do we know that for sure?" Fletcher was tall with a dark, trimmed beard and a gaunt face on top of muscular shoulders and arms. He wore short sleeves and had a tattoo that depicted a revolver blowing out a SoldierBot's CPU.

"Block won't let it hurt us," Nova said. "Relax."

"I'd feel better if that thing were shackled." Fletcher's muscles tensed and his finger rested against the trigger.

"With what? Nothing we have will hold a Mech."

Fletcher's shoulders tensed, but he said nothing. Slowly, he lowered his gun. "Heater and Ferns, I want you on that thing. Watch it at all times. If it does anything sketchy, aim for its chest panel, where the CPU is."

Block's threat indicator surged. "Nova? You promised you wouldn't hurt Oxford."

The saloon's swinging doors slammed open. Helen came running out, arms outstretched, squealing. At the sound of her voice, Wally jerked her head and opened her mouth. Helen nearly knocked Block over when she reached them. Tears streaked her face as she touched Wally's head and kissed her cheeks.

"My sweet girl. You're safe. I was so worried." Helen looked at Block. "Thank you so much for bringing her back safely. You are good, Block."

He nodded, uncertain. He hadn't brought Wally back just for Helen, but humans were odd. Sometimes they said things that didn't make sense—figures of speech. They didn't really mean these things, and yet, they said them anyway.

"May I take her?" Helen asked, searching Block's faceplate.

He didn't want Wally away from him until he figured

out the situation with these troops, but Helen was so excited, he let her lift Wally from the carrier.

"What's she wearing?" Helen asked. "It looks like some kind of metal, yet it's soft."

"Yeah, what is that?" Nova asked.

"One of the robots—my friend—made this suit for Wally. It's armored, bullet resistant. It will keep her safe."

Helen wrinkled her nose. "When was the last time you changed her?"

"It's been several hours."

"I'll take care of it." Helen smiled. "Anything for this girl." She bounced Wally on her hip. "I still have diapers! I've been traveling with things for Wally in case we were... in case we found you." She wiped a tear from her eye. "How do I take this suit off though?"

"There's a button on her collar. The one on the far left will let you take it off." Maxwell had considered everything in his design. "You can take off just the pants. It's two-piece."

Helen carried Wally into the saloon, leaving Block with Nova. He considered the crumbling town, trying to calculate whether the decaying wooden frames were safe enough to withstand another night.

"What is this place? Do you mean to stay?" he asked.

"It's as good a hideout as any for now. We'll have to get moving soon. Once X's troops discover you and Wally are gone, they'll be looking for us."

"Whoa, whoa, whoa!" Fletcher's voice rang out, and someone shrieked.

Block's head swiveled toward the commotion by the stable. Oxford lurched forward, and Nova's troops were about to destroy him.

Chapter 33
She's not responding

Block sprinted over to the men and women guarding Oxford. "Let him be!"

Nova was right behind him. "Weapons down!"

"This thing started to move," Fletcher said.

A woman with short brown hair and silver barrettes said, "It came at us."

"Relax everyone," Nova said.

Block inspected Oxford. He seemed different as he looked around and scanned the people, buildings, and wide-open sky.

"Let's huddle by the saloon," Nova said. "Give Block some time with the Mech."

"And let that thing loose?" Fletcher wasn't giving up.

"It's an order." Nova's eyes narrowed before she led the troops to gather on the saloon steps.

Fletcher never took his eyes off Block and Oxford. His gun didn't leave his hands.

"Block?" Oxford was recognizing him in a new way.

"Hi," Block said. Maxwell had said the device only lasted a few hours.

"Where are we?" Oxford peered at the stable, then scanned the road that led to the saloon. "What happened?"

Block leaned against the stable wall across from Oxford. "I'll tell you everything, but you have to promise you won't be angry."

Oxford shook his head as if rattling internal gears. "I cannot promise that. Tell me anyway. And hurry. There are humans with weapons. The man with the tattoo wants very much to destroy us. So you'd better explain fast."

When Block told Oxford he'd hacked into him with the black box device, the big Mech slammed an arm into the stable's wooden beams, leaving a gaping hole. Across the lane, Fletcher jumped up, rifle ready, but Nova calmed him down.

"How could you betray me?" Oxford's voice boomed, sending a cluster of nearby blackbirds screeching into the air.

"You have to understand, I did it for Wally. You were the only thing that could protect us and let us escape. I activated the device by accident. It rendered you inert, and if I hadn't taken control of you, you would have just been standing there when X's troops entered."

"But if you had never handled the device in the first place, if you had handed it over to me, we would not be in this situation."

Block shifted his feet, annoyed at the little dust plumes he kicked up. "I'm sorry."

"You got what you wanted." Oxford grunted and clenched a fist, ready to strike again, then paused. "Wally is safe, I presume?"

"Yes. She's with a human who cares very much about her. Inside the saloon."

"Wally's safe, and you are not damaged. I'm not damaged. But what about the others? Where's Cybel?"

"When we left, they were under heavy attack. Cybel wanted you to stay and fight."

"But you left anyway?"

Block nodded, knowing this was the part that would make Oxford even angrier.

"You left my soldiers to die?" Oxford rose to his feet, hydraulics straining under his weight. He stomped away from Block and the Western town.

There were shouts from the saloon, but Nova cut them off.

Block followed Oxford, trampling a path through scraggly desert brush. "Oxford, wait."

Oxford slowed, but not much, and Block jogged to catch up. "I'm sorry about what happened. How can I make it right?"

Oxford halted. "First, destroy that device."

"But what if we need it?"

Oxford twisted his massive torso and marched forward.

"Wait, wait! Look." Block held out the device. "I'll destroy it."

Oxford hesitated, and Block tossed the device on the ground, stomping and crushing it under his newly alloyed feet. "There, it's gone. Now can we talk?"

Oxford made a garbled noise that sounded like a grunt.

"I'm sorry we left your army behind. X's troops were bombing on all sides of the canyon. Your troops were barely holding on. I didn't know what to do. I panicked, and I just wanted to get away."

Oxford watched him.

"I'm not as brave as you. Not as strong. I've never even been in a battle before. Well once, but I ran away from it."

The two of them stood together in the open desert, near a saguaro cactus almost as tall as Oxford. A loud tapping—the calling card of a woodpecker—made Block twitch.

"I tried to ping Cybel," Oxford said. "She's not responding."

"Maybe she's busy."

"I can't contact any of my troops. There is nothing but the empty signal of one of the command stations I was hooked into."

"I'm sorry."

"I should've been there for them, fighting along with my army. I know who I am, what I stand for. But you and your wretched device stole that from me. That's why we destroyed those things." Oxford's voice rose like thunder in the desert sky. The bird song ceased. "How would you like it if someone hacked into you and made you something you're not? Made you do things you didn't want to?"

Block lowered his chin. "I wouldn't like that at all."

"There may be nothing left of them. Mach X will be heading this way. He sees what Wally sees, knows where she is. She's tracked."

Block knew as well as Oxford—they had to move.

"Did you tell the humans about Wally?"

Block said nothing.

"Cybel was right about you. I should not have trusted you. You lied to me, and then you hacked me. I would have been better off never having Cybel bring you in. I might still have an army, still have my friends."

Block didn't know what to do. He'd already apologized several times. He'd never had someone as mad at him as Oxford. He didn't like this scenario's outcome.

Not at all.

Oxford plopped himself next to the large cactus and refused to move. Block apologized again, but Oxford didn't respond.

The sun rose higher in the sky, and Block began to worry about Wally—it had been two hours since he'd seen her. He wondered about Nova and the people with her. Did they have fresh drinking water? Was Wally crawling on dirty, flea-infested furniture?

"I have to go back to the town and check on Wally. And I'd better check in with Nova. Let her know we're okay."

Oxford stared at the horizon in stony silence. He might have blended in with the surrounding cactuses if it hadn't been for his tarnished yellow steel, his rectangular edges that defied nature.

"Will you please stay here until I return?" Block asked.

Nothing.

"I have no choice but to go now." Block lingered, watching Oxford for any trace of reaction. There was none, so he walked back in the direction of Nova's hideout. It took him seven minutes to reach the stable, walk past the gaping hole that Oxford had left, and enter the gravel clearing that served as the town's main street. Fletcher sat on the steps of the saloon, wearing a tattered old cowboy hat. His rifle rested on his lap. He bit loudly into an apple and stared as Block approached.

Block scanned the area, looking for Nova and Helen. He was forced to ask Fletcher, "Does Nova happen to be around?"

Fletcher narrowed his eyes, chewing his apple bits loudly.

"I'm sorry. I didn't mean to interrupt while you're eating."

Fletcher swallowed and then spit on the ground. "Man, this thing is bitter. Found it on a tree out back. Nova's in there." He jerked a thumb behind him at the saloon door, but he was in the way.

"May I enter, please?"

Fletcher curled his lip. "I'll be watching you." He grunted and let Block pass.

Block climbed the five rickety steps, old wood bending and creaking under his weight. The stairs would never hold Oxford. The door to the saloon had a divider—two wooden pieces that rested on hinges and swung back and forth. He'd never crossed this kind of door, if you could even call it a door. He nudged the left shutter with one hand and squeezed through, twisting so his back pressed against it. As he crossed the threshold, the light grew dim. His odor register lit up: *Warning, mold and mildew present.*

He decided against night vision; it just wasn't dark enough. Four candles on the tables and one on the bar threw off just enough light to confuse his sensors.

"Hey, Block." Helen sat at a table, bouncing Wally on her knee.

"Hello."

In the corner, the young woman they called Heater stood against the wall with her arms folded. Her jaw tensed at Block. "Where's the Mech?" Her weapon rested against the wall, but she didn't grab for it.

"Oxford is not here. He didn't want to come back."

Nova bounded down a steep, wooden staircase. "Hey. I was wondering when you'd come back." She jumped the last step and landed on the old wooden floorboards with an alarming thud. "I thought we might have to send a search party." She came forward, resting her hands on her hips. "What's going on?"

"Oxford wanted to stay out there. He didn't exactly feel welcome."

"He makes the others nervous. They've only encountered Mechs in battles. You have to understand."

Block didn't really understand. Logic dictated that Oxford had never tried to hurt the humans here, so why would they be ready to destroy him? He didn't want to try to explain this to Nova. It wasn't the right time.

"The thing is, we have to start moving," Block said.

"Why? I know we'll have to move soon, but for right now, this is a good hiding spot."

Oxford's words loomed in Block's memory feed—*Did you tell the humans?* Hiding the truth about Wally's implants had messed up everything in the mine. He didn't want a repeat of the same mistake. And yet, he didn't want Nova and the others to be afraid of Wally. Block trusted Nova and Helen, knew they would never hurt the little girl, but Fletcher was scary. There was no telling what the other strangers would do. Nova couldn't fight all of them on her own.

"Where is Shane?" Block asked.

"I have no idea." Nova bit her lip and crossed her arms. "We parted ways after Hemlock. Shane's army was crippled after the battle." She stared down at the floor. It was coated with sawdust, much to Block's dismay. "I was wrong. I'm sorry for tricking you." She addressed a spot on the floor, but Block calculated that she meant the message for him. "I'm sorry for not listening to you. Not trusting you. I should have been spending more time with you instead of isolating you in the basement and telling you to keep out of everyone's way."

The others were quiet. Wally chewed on her knuckles, watching their conversation with wide eyes.

"I want to help you now." Nova looked up, finally shifting her attention to Block. "I want to make things right and help you protect Wally. That's what I should have been doing all along."

Block's timing was terrible, but Nova would find out sooner or later. "I have something to tell you," he said. "It's important. And you're not going to like it."

Chapter 34
What's the point?

Nova shifted her feet and tensed her shoulders. "Okay, I'm listening."

Block glanced at Wally and Helen. Heater lingered in the corner, watching.

"Hey, everyone, can you give me and Block a few minutes alone, please?" Nova asked.

Heater flinched as she passed Block. Helen carried Wally who reached her pudgy arms out and said, "Bwock."

"Her first word," Helen said.

Nova smiled for the briefest of moments. "What do you know? Wally's first word is Block. We'll be out soon, Helen. Thanks."

"No problem." Helen jostled Wally in her arms as they left.

"What is it, Block? What's so important?"

"I should've told you at Hemlock when I discovered it, but I was concerned for Wally's safety."

Tiny wrinkle lines appeared on Nova's forehead. "You know whatever it is, you can tell me."

He regarded her. "Yes, I know you want to help. My primary directive is to protect Wally. Do whatever it takes to keep her safe. I processed many scenarios and chose to keep her secret."

Nova scratched the back of her neck. Her body temperature rose three tenths of a degree. "What secret?"

"Mach X implanted something in her brain. For reasons that are not clear, X can see and hear what Wally does."

Nova's jaw went slack. "What are you talking about? That's not possible."

"I didn't think the tech existed either, but I have files that prove it from the machine that housed her when I discovered her. It passed me encrypted files."

"What does that mean, that Mach X sees and hears what she does?" She shook her head. "She's just a baby."

"I know it's difficult to accept."

She dug her nails into her scalp. "Are you saying this whole time, even back at Hemlock, Mach X was watching us?"

"And hearing us."

Nova paced over to an old battered table. "Shane kept going on and on about a spy. I thought he was just being paranoid. He was right." Her vocal cords were tight.

Block had wondered if he would feel something different after telling the truth. Humans sometimes said they felt relieved to get something off their chest. His chest still weighed the same.

Nova's eyes shifted wildly as she processed the revelation. "So that's how Mach X has been tracking you and Wally. The thing knows we're here now."

"Yes, I suspect it's able to lock onto her coordinates or gather information from the surroundings."

"Why would an AI do this to a baby?"

"I'm not sure."

"So, what do we do?" Her arms flailed. It was rare to see her so uncertain.

"First, tell no one about Wally. Not even Helen," he said. "If your soldiers find out, they might hurt her."

She folded her arms. "They wouldn't hurt a baby." She paused. "I don't think they would."

"Well, we can't take the risk. I chose to tell you, and you alone."

"Okay. Then what?"

"You have to go away. Keep Wally moving until we figure out how to help her. Mach X's troops could already be on their way."

She exhaled so sharply, a whistle burst forth from her lips. "Right. I'll get everyone to pack and we can move out in an hour." She narrowed her eyes. "Wait a minute, what are you planning to do?"

"I have to do a favor for a friend that I wronged. I'll take care of the situation and then come join you."

"Is it something with the Mech? Where is that thing, by the way?"

"Oxford is not far, but I wronged him. I held back the truth and there were consequences. His army, his friends were hurt."

"It's over. The damage is already done. You should come with us."

"I'll join you as soon as possible, but I need to go back to the mine with Oxford."

"You're sure about this? What if the SoldierBots are still there, guarding the mine?"

"Oxford will deal with them. He got us out of there.

He can get us back in. If any of his robots are still fighting, Oxford wants to help them, and I should help him."

Nova looked at him in a strange way. Eyes glistening, she rested her hand on his shoulder. "You're a good..." She bit back her words and shook her head. "Wow, I almost said person. You are... good."

He wasn't exactly sure what she was trying to say, but it was nice to hear a compliment. "Thank you."

"Use the comm pin to keep me informed of your status. We'll rendezvous after you take care of this. I'll get the others ready to move out." She strode away, then spun on her heels. "Is there something we should do with Wally? Blindfold or put earmuffs on her?"

"It won't matter," Block said. "X will still find her. When you discuss plans or strategy, do it where she can't hear."

"Got it." She walked out on the saloon steps. "Everyone, pack up. We clear out in one hour!"

Fletcher and Heater leaned against the old cantina in a patch of shade, sharing a cigarette. He whined, "What? I thought we were camped out here."

"Change of plans," Nova said. "Get moving. This is not a joke."

Fletcher, Heater, and the man named Ferns moved slowly and scowled.

Block shuffled onto the saloon patio next to Nova. "How many troops do you have?"

"It's them and five others. They're camped out in other buildings."

"That's it?" Block had expected her to have more of an army.

"Shane and I didn't part on good terms. Let's just say I

was lucky to get this many." She leaned against the wooden post. "Sorry you aren't more impressed."

"It's fine. We have a Mech and possibly more robots from the mine can help us."

"Are you sure about that? Why would they help us?"

"Many of them got to meet Wally."

She straightened. "Enough said."

Block trekked away from the town, returning to the coordinates where he'd left Oxford. New scenarios sprang forth—what if Oxford had left?—but the massive metal giant was still sitting next to the towering saguaro.

"I brought you something," Block said. Nova had pointed him to an old shed behind the abandoned buildings. After scrounging together some rusting oil cans, he found just enough to give him and Oxford additional power. Block rested his backpack on the ground and began to take out cans. He handed one to Oxford. "Here you go."

"What are you doing here?"

"Helping you." Block pulled out more cans. Most of them rattled and were half empty, but there were seven. He waited, expecting Oxford to grab one. But the big robot just sat there.

"You must be pretty drained," Block said. "Go ahead, take one."

"What's the point?"

Block hadn't expected that reply. The Oxford he knew had been commanding, sure, and confident. He had a powerful presence. This Oxford seemed rusty and helpless. Had the hacking changed Oxford permanently?

Block didn't want to sit in the dirt. He spied large black ants scurrying around the cans he'd set down. With Oxford sitting down, Block was finally level to his face.

"Everything is the point," Block said. "Fuel up. We're going back." In the bright sunlight, Block noticed the tarnish in Oxford's faded yellow chrome and resisted the impulse to buff it.

"Here." Block thrust a can at him.

"I want to deplete here in this spot."

"No. I won't allow that."

Oxford said nothing.

"I'm very sorry I wronged you," Block said. "It is one of the biggest mistakes of my existence. Second only to the death of my former employer."

Oxford bent his head slightly, the first movement he'd made since Block had arrived.

"I want to help you set this right. I sent Nova, Wally, and the others ahead. Nova knows the truth about Wally. They're on the move."

"You told them? Good."

"I realized it's no use keeping secrets, and I shouldn't have kept one from you. It was a mistake in my decision logic."

"You cost me everything."

"I know, and I'm sorry. We go back and find Cybel and help the others."

"Too late."

"We don't know that for sure. Your communications were cut. Maybe there was a signal interruption or faulty equipment."

"In all of my troops at the same time? Unlikely."

"We have to go back and make things right." Block kicked the dirt under his feet. "You sitting here and running out of fuel—that is not the answer. Imagine if your troops saw you like this."

Oxford shifted just a millimeter, enough for Block to notice.

"What would they think about you? That you gave up? That you didn't want to go back and see if they survived? When we left LB and Maxwell, they were still in the mine. Maxwell was damaged, but still there. They were setting traps. I bet they survived."

The wind picked up and hissed in Block's auditory sensors. A tiny dust tornado swirled up, blasting sand against their steel parts.

Finally Oxford moved his arm and opened the panel in his side where his feeding tube was located.

"Fuel me up," he said.

Chapter 35
We wait them out

After they'd drained the oil cans, Oxford and Block headed south toward the mine. Block clung to Oxford's back as the Mech strode along the flat, straight highway that led all the way into Mexico. Block thought about Wally, strapped in a carrier either on his back or chest during their journeys. Now he could understand what she saw. It was weird to be carried by something much larger than you.

Every time one of Oxford's enormous feet struck the ground, Block's entire frame shook. His threat level indicator warned him there could be damage, but Block wasn't about to stop Oxford. This was the fastest way to reach the mine and see whether there were any survivors. Block had worked hard to convince Oxford, and he hoped it was the right thing.

Oxford slowed his gait and stared at something in the distance.

Block adjusted his hold around Oxford's neck and scanned the road ahead. "What is it? Why did you stop?"

"Something flashed in the distance. We must get off

the road." Oxford veered sideways and sprinted into the desert brush that lined the highway. There were no tall trees, nothing that would hide a twelve-foot-tall combat Mech with a CleanerBot hanging on his back. He kept running west, away from the highway.

"What are you doing?" Block asked, and when Oxford didn't respond he shouted and waved his hand in front of Oxford's face. "Why are you going this way?"

"Get out of view."

Block swiveled his head to see what was happening back on the highway. Something bright and shiny reflected in the sunlight. He zoomed in as far as he could and glimpsed a convoy in the distance—armored SUVs, two spider combat Mechs, drones, and SoldierBots marching in formation.

"It's them!" Block said.

"No kidding. That's why we got off the highway. I can't fight all of them by myself."

"What do we do? What if they see us?"

"Cloak your comms." Oxford halted.

Block released his grip and slid down Oxford's back.

"Get down and lay low." Oxford's hydraulics hissed as he folded his legs beneath him, then lowered his armored torso to the ground in an attempt to lay down on the sun-baked soil.

Block flattened out. He would be hidden, but the Mech could be spotted.

"We wait them out," Oxford said.

Mach X's army was headed north and would know Wally's location. By now, Nova and the others would have moved out of the Old West town. He hoped they were far enough ahead of this convoy.

"I need to warn Nova."

"Not now," Oxford said. "Wait until they pass. If they detect your signal, they'll discover and destroy us."

So they waited. The convoy was ten school buses long.

Block asked quietly, "Did you know there were that many?"

"I knew their force was large. We prepared for a long time, but it wasn't enough."

After twenty minutes, the cluster of troops had passed. Oxford rose to his knees, watching until they fell out of sight.

"Can I message Nova now?" Block asked.

"Make it quick." Oxford rose. "Then we move."

Block tapped the Ghostbusters pin and switched on his comms. "Nova, come in. It's me. Block."

A few seconds passed before she responded. *I'm here.* Her breathing was heavy.

"We went south on the highway and Mach X's troops just passed by. We hid from them."

Let me guess, they're headed our way?

"Correct. There were too many, even for Oxford to fight. There were drones, spider WarBots, and Soldier-Bots, of course."

Awesome. Do you have any good *news for me?*

Block processed her question and looked around. He really didn't grasp anything good about their situation.

That was a joke. He knew her eyes were rolling. *What's your next step?*

"We're heading for the mine to locate survivors. We're not far."

Oxford stared in the direction of the mine, presumably searching for signals from his army, searching for any sign of robot life.

Understood. We keep moving. Now that the SoldierBot army is after us, we'll get no rest.

A scenario occurred to Block. "Hold on a moment, Nova." He muted himself and asked Oxford, "If they found a cave or somewhere underground, is it possible Wally's signal would be interrupted?"

"No. They detected her in the mineshaft."

"But what if they could find a way to block her signal somehow? Cloak her like we do ourselves, would that work?"

"Perhaps. We would need someone who understood design. Hurry this up, we don't have much time."

Block resumed comms with Nova. "Sorry, I was just working on an idea with Oxford."

What kind of idea?

"Thinking of how we could cloak Wally's signal so you could move and not be tracked."

And? What did you come up with?

"We would need an engineer. Someone skilled in communications technology."

Right. Fat chance of that.

"Are you familiar with the Faraday cage?"

I've heard of it. What are you getting at? He sensed a pitch to Nova's voice. He recognized it as irritation.

"If you can find aluminum foil or sheets of aluminum, perhaps it would interrupt the signals—"

Oxford's head jerked sideways. He shifted as if preparing for an attack. "Block, now!"

Whoa! What was that? Nova asked.

"Interference," Block said. "We have to go."

Wait—

But he cut her off and sprinted after Oxford who had started running. "Hey, let me get on your back." Oxford slowed just enough for Block to scramble up onto his back and grasp his neck.

"What happened?" Block asked.

"I got a ping from the mine."

Something surged in Block's processor. He'd been right. A survivor.

Oxford's legs pumped against the ground, much faster than before.

"Who was it?" Block asked.

"Cybel. She's still there."

Chapter 36
Commit this to your memory cloud

Oxford sprinted at fifty miles per hour, his full-speed pace. They reached the winding dirt road in twenty minutes, but there was a problem. The departing army had kicked up so much dust, it still hung in the air like a fog. Not only that, large boulders and rock piles now littered the narrow road, no doubt disturbed by the robot army's massive bulk and sheer number.

"It's difficult to navigate," Oxford said. "We'll have to go slower."

Block peered over Oxford's shoulder. He could barely make out the obstacles. "Let me down. I can help navigate."

Oxford halted and Block scrambled down. On solid ground, nearer to the road, Block could more easily pick out a path. "Follow me," he said, leading the way.

Oxford grunted agreement and picked up his pace while Block jogged, swerving to avoid rock piles that were as big as him. As Oxford followed, he kicked the rubble aside, sending rocks careening off the cliff's edge.

"Faster!" Oxford commanded.

"I'm going as fast as I can." The visibility wasn't great. Even night vision couldn't help Block in this situation. His only advantage was being lower to the ground than Oxford.

After many minutes, the rock-dust haze finally lifted, and they reached the opening to the canyon. Dozens more boulders lay strewn across the ground than Block's memory cloud revealed from his prior escape. Thick coils of black smoke floated past them. Block's threat indicator lit up—somewhere nearby, a fire burned.

Oxford bolted forward and leaped onto an enormous boulder that jutted up from the desert bed. He perched there, rotating his head to scan the canyon floor. Block stepped onto a small boulder and spread his arms wide to steady himself. He couldn't leap to great heights like Oxford could. Instead, he had to pick his way among flat-topped rocks, careful not to get his new feet trapped in a hole or crevasse.

Oxford jumped down from his vantage point atop the boulder and sprinted ahead. Oxford hadn't said a word about his plans, and Block wondered if he should've kept riding on his back. As it was, he was advancing at the pace of a desert tortoise compared to Oxford's maneuverability. CleanerBots just weren't built for rugged terrain.

Block had just managed to clear the biggest wall of rocks when he kicked the severed head of a FactoryBot. He halted and drew his arms across his chest. He was so used to protecting Wally, but she wasn't there. The robot's head rolled five feet away before it struck a rock. Tattered circuits and wires snaked from its neck. He stepped closer. The head had been separated cleanly—wires had been snipped off neatly, perhaps the result of a sharp-edged blade.

But where was the rest of the body? He looked up and saw Oxford in the distance, nearing flames that rose high and licked the canyon's sheer walls.

"Be careful," Block shouted. But that was silly. Oxford could protect himself. He didn't need a CleanerBot telling him what to do. Still, it was in Block's nature to be cautious. What if they were about to be ambushed by SoldierBots left behind to destroy or capture them?

Oxford would know what to do. He could defend against practically anything. "Over here," he yelled.

"I'm coming." Block jogged forward, but his foot got caught in a patch of rubble. He staggered forward, waving his arms to steady himself, but it was no use. He crashed down on his left knee, then his right. His chest hit something hard and metal and hot. His bracing hands clanged against the scorched side of a Spider-WarBot. Block reared back. His threat level indicator was skyrocketing: *Warning, warning.*

A pulsating red light flashed inside the SpiderBot's visor. The thing was still awake. SpiderBots could shoot laser weapons, not to mention bot-killing machine gun cannons.

The damaged Bot had spotted Block and was about to make him into Swiss cheese. Block scooted backward on his knees and raised his hands in surrender. "Please, don't shoot. I mean no harm."

The SpiderBot watched, its pulsating light scanning him. One of its long, intact steel tendrils unfurled and landed on Block's shoulder, wrapped around his neck, and yanked him forward. Block was caught. He reached up, trying to loosen the steel coil, but his digits weren't a match for the solid steel tentacle. The SpiderBot squeezed.

"Oxford!" Block shouted. He was answered by a loud crashing noise from where Oxford was. Was something attacking him too?

Block struggled against the SpiderBot's rogue arm. The machine pulled him so close, his head rested against the SpiderBot's smoldering underbelly. Block readied the only weapon he had—the blade on his palm that he used to saw things or open Wally's food cans. He ejected the knife and reached up to hit the Bot in its faceplate, but his knife bent and sheared off against the armored helmet. The blade clattered to the ground.

Block's threat indicator buzzed in his feed: *Threat level 10. Red Alert. Immediate action needed.*

He had only one option. "I'll clean you," he said. He'd gotten out of more than one dangerous situation this way.

But the SpiderBot kept squeezing and would soon crush him to a point where his CPU would be destroyed, and his microbial stomach would release all its contents.

Block opened his back panel and released several extensions at once: his vacuum tube, compressed air, and one other tube. He pushed them all up, ordering them to clean—what other choice did he have?—and let them blindly go about their routines. One of the steel tubes twisted around and cracked the SpiderBot's visor, jamming itself inside. Still trapped against the underbelly, Block sent a stream of disinfectant spray into the Bot's helmet at full blast.

The enemy robot shuddered so violently, Block thought there might have been an earthquake. Loose dust kicked up, blinding him for a few seconds. Then the creature stilled. Its grip on Block's neck loosened, and Block threw off the tentacle.

He scrambled away on all fours. The red beam in the SpiderBot's visor had gone dark. Block stowed away all his cleaning apparatuses and raced toward Oxford. He needed to stay close to the Mech. Other enemies could still be alive, and like the SpiderBot, able to kill. But if he ran too fast, he would risk another fall. So Block commanded himself to slow. A hundred feet away, Oxford was shooting a large stream of water from his arm at something on fire.

"Oxford!" But then Block realized shouting might alert still-sentient enemy robots. He stopped himself and concentrated on navigating the precarious gravel under his feet. He sidestepped mangled robot parts, spotting the legs of a SoldierBot and the exploded bits of robot innards he couldn't identify. He couldn't avoid the crunch of downed drones that lay scattered in pieces. Much of the canyon's face had been scorched black. Block passed the entrance to the mine. Something had fractured and ripped apart the rock above, so the tunnel's mouth was now crammed full of rubble from a landslide. An enemy SUV had crashed down from the cliffs above and landed on its roof. The tires had melted, and the vehicle still smoldered.

Block ran to Oxford who was extinguishing an armored SUV—Ahtron. After dousing the flames, the car's armor was still halfway down, shielding the windows and roof. The undercarriage was dripping from the deluge. Splotchy black orbs that looked like puddles of melted wax occupied the places where the tires had once been.

"Ahtron?" Block called out.

There was no answer from the intelligent vehicle. Oxford bent down and slammed his fist against the roof. "Open."

Nothing happened. Was Ahtron so utterly damaged? Completely dead?

"Cybel's inside." Oxford rammed his fist against the shielded windows. The impervious armor dented and then pushed itself back out. Oxford reached underneath and lifted the entire vehicle four feet, then dropped it. Metal screeched against hard earth as the vehicle absorbed the shock, but Ahtron still didn't open.

"How do you know she's inside?" Block asked.

"She is pinging me. She's in there. I need to get her out. The SUV is destroyed, and it's gone into full lock-down mode—a last resort so as not to let enemies hack into its brains."

"But, if you continue to pummel and drop it, you're going to hurt Cybel, right?"

"I can't think of any other way."

If Ahtron was no longer functioning at all—if he was truly destroyed—even the hacking device wouldn't have worked. No matter, since Oxford had forced Block to destroy the device anyway.

Oxford kicked the vehicle, and it rocked from side to side.

"May I try something?" Block asked.

"We can't waste time." Oxford smashed down on the roof of the car with both fists. This time, the SUV's roof crunched halfway down and took longer to rebound, popping back like a chewing gum bubble.

Oxford was about to smash Ahtron again but tilted his head. He backed up, lowering his arms.

"What is it?" Block asked.

"Cybel is damaged. Continuing to try and break the car will hurt her more." Oxford twisted his torso and stomped in a circle, summoning a spiraling dust cloud. "I don't know what to do."

It was the first time Block had ever heard Oxford admit uncertainty.

"Perhaps there is something I can try," Block offered.

Oxford grabbed a boulder the size of Block and hurled it in the direction of the mine. "You're a CleanerBot, I'm a Mech. If I can't get into the car and help Cybel escape, nobody can."

He was furious. After hurling three more rocks, he picked up a battered SoldierBot, swung its body in a wide arc, and tossed it on top of the cliff. Its heavy metal frame screeched against boulders as it slid.

While Oxford rampaged, Block inched toward Ahtron. He placed his hand on the vehicle's hood and said quietly, "I hope you rest in peace, Ahtron."

Oxford had crossed to the mine entrance and started digging his way through the barrier, tossing rocks, rubble, and boulders aside as easily as one digging through a closet to find a pair of shoes.

"I don't know if there's still some piece of you that is sentient," Block continued, "but if you open enough to let Cybel out, I'll give you that buff and shine that I promised."

Block waited, hoping something would happen. At The Drake, he'd occasionally been dispatched to pick locks using his tools and circuitry. It was rare when guests locked themselves in their rooms or employees had accidentally changed the codes, but it had happened. But on Ahtron's model, there were no locks to pick. The SUV was fully automated.

Block's hand still rested on the hood and something tingled in his hand's circuitry as if a surge of electricity had passed into his hand. "Ahtron?"

The armor on Ahtron's side began to shimmer and fade. After a moment, the door handle was revealed along with the window. Cybel sat hunched over in the front passenger seat.

"Oxford!" Block shouted. "Come here quickly." But the Mech was furiously digging away at the mine entrance.

Block sprinted over. "Oxford!" The Mech ignored him and nearly took his head off with a rock until Block began waving his arms.

Oxford hesitated, a boulder the size of a car in his arms.

"I got in. Cybel is there."

Oxford twisted his torso and tossed the rock aside, which shook the ground under their feet. He bounded over to the SUV. Cybel didn't look good. Her body was twisted to one side inside the vehicle. Oxford bent and scooped her out. He set her on the ground. Her lower half —below what would've been a waist on a human being— was gone.

Oxford sank to his knees beside her. "Cybel, can you hear me? It's Oxford."

Her torso twitched. Her voice rose from her voice box, though it crackled. "Ox." She raised her head to look at them. A wide crack ran along her visor, revealing raw metal circuitry beneath. "Is that Block?"

"Yes, it's me." Block shifted his feet in the sand.

"You got me out," she said. "Well done, CleanerBot."

"What happened to you?" Oxford asked.

"There were too many. Far more than we'd expected."

Her voice not only cracked, it trembled. Damaged auditory circuits.

Block noted the steel cables and advanced mesh circuitry nodes that now lay in ragged tangles in her abdomen. Massive damage had been done to her microbial fuel tank. Dark, viscous fluid leaked from her gaping cavity.

She took longer than usual to form her words. "You damaged my comm on that last crack you made at Ahtron."

"I'm sorry about that," Oxford said. "I didn't know what else to do. I should have given Block a chance." Oxford hesitated. "Any other survivors?"

"Not out here," she said. "Maybe in the mine. I don't know."

"We'll conduct a search and take you and any survivors with us," Oxford said. "We'll get you somewhere safe and fix you. I'll rebuild my army, take my revenge."

"Leave me." Cybel reached out and wrapped her fist around one of his fingers. "This is no way to exist."

"You're coming with us. There's no question," Oxford said. "Your value is immeasurable. You're an asset."

"I failed. Big time. Look around you."

"You made a stand," Oxford said. "I'm sorry I wasn't here. It wasn't my choice."

"Good that..." Whatever Cybel tried to say next was garbled. "You'd been here, you'd be a pile of metal. Good you got away. SpiderBot severed me with a blade. But I got it. I took it down."

"I'll fix you, then rebuild my army."

Block couldn't stop staring at Cybel's mangled torso,

and she noticed. "Commit this to your memory cloud, CleanerBot," she said. "This is what happens in war."

Block stared down at his feet.

"There was a new kind of robot here," she continued. "A NannyBot, only one like I'd never seen before. It was taller, stronger. It looked capable of fighting."

"But NannyBots are harmless, meant for childcare." Oxford said.

"It pinged me, said to surrender the human baby, but by then you were gone. There was something else. The NannyBot claimed it was Mach X."

"X was here?" Oxford asked. "But that's impossible."

Even Block knew that the supercomputer maintained its CPU in a secret, high-security vault in New York City. It was assumed that Mach X's troops and commanders carried out its actions in various cities and waged war against humans. X was always commanding from afar, safe where its core processor was fully protected.

Cybel shuddered like a surge overtook her. "Perhaps X is becoming free of constraints—able to move about using other sentient beings like this NannyBot."

"Like the child's implants," Oxford said.

Block raised his hands against his chest. There was no threat indicator warning, yet he felt exposed somehow. An odd sensation churned deep in his circuitry. He knew what Cybel was getting at. "X is becoming something else. More than an AI."

"Why?" Oxford asked. "I've never heard of a technology where an AI can be in more than one place."

"X wants to be in many places at once. It wants to see and hear as a human does," Block said. "That's what X is doing with Wally. According to the Incubator's file, there's more than one child. Perhaps there are several more."

Cybel's strained voice chimed in. "Mach X wants to control the human child." She paused with an uncontrollable twitch. "Perhaps many humans. Maybe all of them."

Chapter 37
The XC13r recoding maneuver

There were no other survivors outside. Cybel laid on the ground where Oxford had left her. Block tried to help when Oxford started burrowing into the wall of debris and rockslide that covered the tunnel entrance by moving a few rocks at a time, but Oxford said, "Stay away. I'm faster without you, and I don't want to hit you by accident."

It was true, so Block didn't argue. He drifted back to where Cybel rested against a boulder.

"What else did the NannyBot, I mean X, say to you?" Block asked.

"It said that if we handed over the human baby they would leave. That we'd be spared." She paused, her voice waves breaking. "I said that was impossible since the baby wasn't even here. I don't know if X knew that you'd left or not. They decided to destroy us anyway."

"I'm sorry I took Oxford away."

"I'm glad you did. He'd be dead right now too. I should be. You should have left me inside Ahtron. I would have run out of fuel. Expired. The way it should have been. Now look at me."

Block didn't want to look any more at Cybel's mangled abdomen. Instead, he stared in Oxford's direction and watched as the Mech flung boulders aside as if they were merely cardboard boxes. He didn't know what to say to Cybel.

"Listen to me, CleanerBot. End this right now. Stick a blade through my CPU."

"But that would destroy you." Block backed up a step.

"Quickly, before Oxford returns. Blame it on something else—mangled wiring that shorted me out."

Block looked at Oxford. He was almost done clearing space for them to pass into the mine.

"Now," Cybel demanded. "I can't do it myself, or I would. My programming forbids self-destruction unless enemies are attacking."

Block backed up another step. Why was she putting this on him?

"Do it. This is what I want."

Block shook his head. "I can't."

"Do it for the code of honor. Look, I'm begging you."

Block had never had to deal with a suicidal robot. This was too much for his simple processor.

Lumbering footsteps signaled Oxford's approach. "The tunnel is clear. We can enter and look for survivors. Cybel, I'm bringing you inside with us." He scooped her up and walked toward the mine. "Can't leave you alone out here."

As he carried her, she looked at Block. Her visor hid any emotion, but he knew she was angry with him, even worse than before. Should he tell Oxford what she'd said? That might complicate things, and anyway, it was done.

He hadn't done it, and this would be the last of it, he hoped.

Block followed them inside and switched on his night vision. Too late. He stumbled and landed on something heavy. He stared into the visor of a SoldierBot, then rose to his knees and glimpsed another body, then another. He stood and scanned the ground, counting sixteen mangled SoldierBots and eight FactoryBots.

Oxford surveyed the scene. "My troops made a valiant last stand."

"I don't understand," Block said. "They don't show any signs of damage. No laser damage or bullet holes."

"EMP burst," Cybel said.

Oxford said, "We scavenged an e-bomb from the humans. We'd been saving it for something that really mattered. And this did."

"But it destroyed your own troops too?" Block considered what Cybel had said, that she could self-destroy only if under attack.

"They knew what it meant," Oxford said. "Let's go." He bounded deeper into the tunnel and Block followed. He sent a ping, searching for LB and Maxwell. He wasn't surprised when there was no answer.

And yet, there was no sign of warfare deeper in the mine. Things rested in places as they had before. No evidence of detonations or gunfire. Perhaps Mach X's troops hadn't made it past the entrance. LB and Maxwell would have been protected unless they'd been destroyed by the EMP too. "How far does the EMP blast go?"

"I would estimate a radius of three hundred feet in any direction," Oxford said.

The hall where he'd left LB and Maxwell was farther

than that. Block's processor busied, wanting to pick and choose the scenarios where they had survived.

After a minute, they reached the elevator. Oxford went to grab the hand crank, but Block stopped him. "Don't touch it. It was damaged in our escape." Block looked down where he'd seen Maxwell's body fall. The robot was gone.

The elevator bed rested at the bottom, four stories down. So, LB had made it!

"How can we get down?" Block asked.

"I can jump it." Oxford held Cybel in his arms. "Get on my back." He knelt down. Block scrambled up and grasped his neck in a bear hug.

Oxford leaped down and landed with a thud that resounded through the chamber. His hydraulics were so powerful they absorbed the shock. Even clinging to Oxford's back, Block had bounced upon impact and was still okay. But he was glad Wally wasn't here. It would've been too dangerous for her. He let go and dropped down, calling out, "LB! Maxwell! Hey, it's Block and Oxford."

And then Block spied the outline of something on the dusty ground. An object had been dragged into the great room. He followed it. "LB?"

Block entered the great room, which was eerily empty and devoid of the constant clanking and hammering. His eyes adjusted to the dim light on the wall, and then he saw Maxwell. The robot's back was facing him. He sat on his workbench hunched over something.

"Maxwell!" Block shouted and sprinted over. He halted when he saw Maxwell's project. LB's head and torso had been crushed. Maxwell wore a visor with a bright light that shone down. With fine tweezers, he worked on LB's CPU.

"Maxwell, what happened?" Block asked. Oxford and Cybel lingered nearby, quiet.

"I'm in a delicate operation here." The usual playful tone of Maxwell's voice had disappeared.

"I see that. Is LB going to be okay?"

"I'm attempting to rewire his CPU. It was damaged in the crash."

"Crash?"

"LB succeeded in getting the elevator down, only it crushed him. Now if I can just get this wire to connect over here..."

Maxwell was so intently focused, Block said nothing so as not to disturb him. He waited for something to happen—LB to flicker to life or twitch or buzz—but nothing did.

"Maxwell"—Block stepped forward—"how long have you been working on LB?"

"Nine hours, fourteen minutes, and thirty-two seconds."

Block edged closer. "Are you okay?"

"I suffered some damage in the fall, but I'll be fine. I haven't tried the XC13r recoding maneuver yet. That's my next step."

Block let him attempt the fix. LB's warped body failed to stir.

Finally, Block rested a hand on Maxwell's shoulder. "He's not coming back. You did everything you could."

Maxwell paused, grasping the tweezers in his metal fingers.

"He would be so proud of you," Block said. "It's time to let him rest."

"Rest? You mean, let him rust here with the others?"

The instruments fell from Maxwell's fingers and clattered to the table.

"I mean, it's time we let him go. Oxford is here, and we found Cybel. We have a place to go. We'll bring you with us."

"But LB stayed behind to save me," Maxwell said.

"I know. I was here when it happened. But I know LB. I used to work with him in Chicago, remember? He would want you to carry on and come travel with us. I know it."

"You think he would want that?" Maxwell asked.

"I'm sure of it."

Chapter 38
All of us

They buried LB in the desert on top of a small hill overlooking the valley. It was easy for Oxford to scoop out a grave and set LB's battered body into it. The setting sun scattered bright orange and yellow crescent waves.

After explaining the human tradition of funerals that he'd seen in movies, Block offered to say a few words. "LB was always kind to me. He was nice to everyone at The Drake. LB did his job efficiently and with purpose—cleaning thousands of sheets and towels every week." Block paused as the evening breeze swept past. "But I think what really brought LB happiness was finding all of you. Maxwell, you were his best friend, and he looked up to Oxford. He told me so. And Cybel too." Block didn't really know if the part about Cybel was true, but he didn't want to make her feel left out. "Now we'll have a moment of silence."

Oxford grumbled. "What is the purpose?"

"I saw it in the movies. The humans just stand there and are silent for thirty seconds. You're supposed to think about the person who died."

Cybel twitched from where she'd been placed on the ground.

"Let's get on with it then," Oxford said.

"And now we'll have a moment of silence," Block repeated to make it official. He started a thirty-second timer in his feed. In that time, he retrieved memory flashes of LB. Would some part of LB's consciousness still ramble about inside the metal circuitry of his body? One day the same thing would happen to him, and Block hoped there would be someone around to give him a moment of silence.

"Okay." Block shuffled his feet. "That was thirty seconds."

Maxwell had been still and quiet through the whole ceremony. He bowed to Block. "Thank you. I've never been to a funeral before or witnessed one. It was a nice way to say goodbye to my friend."

"You're welcome."

The ragtag group marched into the desert, heading north on the highway.

"Can you fix her?" Oxford asked after several minutes spent trekking along the dark highway. Night was settling in. Coyotes howled in the distance, crickets chirped, and the darkness seemed to swallow up the dry earth that stretched all around the four robots.

"I'll try my best." Maxwell lugged a box of tools he'd grabbed before exiting the mine. The FactoryBot had a wide dent in his lower left side that he said would easily mend. "I can definitely manage her voicebox and comm repairs. No problem."

"And her legs?" Oxford asked.

"We can probably scavenge something along the—"

"No," Cybel said. "I will not be mashed onto cheap,

tin FactoryBot legs. Or worse, the bottom half of a CleanerBot."

They marched on in silence. Block assumed Cybel would be grateful for any kind of legs at all—to have mobility again, rather than be carried. But then again, what did he know? Her model was sleek and advanced. Other robot parts might not even work with hers.

He tapped his Ghostbusters pin and reached out to Nova for the third time. She hadn't answered yet. He figured she must be sleeping. "Nova, come in. It's Block, are you there?" Only the gritty chorus of chirping toads answered. His logic processor scrambled to grasp scenarios. She could have lost her pin. It might have fallen off in their scramble to leave the camp or when they hiked into the foothills.

"She's not answering," Oxford said. "How do we find them?"

"I'm not sure," Block said. "I suppose we head back to the Old West town and look for clues."

"That place will be overrun with Mach X's troops by now," Oxford said.

"I'm not sure what else to do," Block said, and Oxford grunted in reply.

"The humans' need to sleep is a major disadvantage," Cybel said. "X's troops will keep advancing, never stopping."

She was right. Nova and her troops could probably do without rest for one or two nights, but Helen and Wally were not equipped to travel long distances on no sleep.

Block looked at Maxwell. "When we find them, will you design a way to shield the signals from Wally's brain implant?"

"I'll start crunching on how that would work on a

human," he said. "Keep in mind, I've never worked on humans before. Can I drill into her brain?"

"Absolutely not!" Block's threat indicator buzzed. "You can't do anything that could break her skin or hurt her or electrocute her."

"Okay. That narrows down the possibilities."

The clanking of their feet along the asphalt echoed in the night. Block tapped the pin that connected him to Nova and waited for the familiar soft fizz to indicate she was tuning in. He would sacrifice a circuit node to hear her voice at that moment, anything to know that she and Wally were all right.

Still, no reply.

Block would stick to the plan and head to their last known location. Nova would have left some kind of clue —she was a master of hiding and fighting against robots. She'd find a way to keep Wally safe. He just knew it, deep in his circuitry, as sure as he counted on the wires, chips, and sensors that gave him sentience.

Many hours passed, and a pale orange hue shimmered in the east, teasing the dark away. Block processed and churned on scenarios and plans as the sun edged up over the horizon. He halted, and the others kept going another twenty feet before Maxwell noticed Block's absence. "Hey, why'd you stop?"

Oxford pivoted and tilted his head. In his arms, Cybel's visor reflected rose-hued wisps of early light.

"We're going to keep Wally safe," Block said. "Together. All of us." They had advantages: Oxford's gigantic limbs, Cybel's military brains that could outwit X's troops, and Maxwell's extraordinary engineering abilities.

Block marched on and the others followed. He wasn't

exactly sure what his place in their group was. After all, he wasn't strong or particularly smart, and he didn't have a special skill other than caring for Wally and cleaning places.

He needed to offer something else to the group, a role deserving of their help.

His processor seized on a job in a millisecond. He was their guide in this unusual mission—the one to remind them what it was all about—saving Wally.

Block perceived a tingling rise from his core. Maybe this was what he was always meant to do—guide and protect.

For the first time ever, he decided he was worthy of the job.

Block's story continues . . .

Dear Reader,

Thanks for reading *Steel Defender*! Are you ready to find out what's next for Block? Book 3: *Steel Protector* is next in the series.

If you enjoyed Block's journey, I invite you to read his journal logs from Chicago. You'll discover what happened in the days before the Uprising and how the aftermath affected him and others at the hotel. It's a page-turner you don't want to miss.

You can download *STEEL APOCALYPSE* (*A Robot's Journal*) for free by visiting: CameronCoral.com/Block Journal

Enjoy,

Cameron Coral

P.S. - Did you enjoy this book? I'd love a review wherever you purchased this book if you have a few minutes. Thank you kindly because reviews mean a lot to me. They show me you want me to keep writing, and they help other readers discover my books.

Also by Cameron Coral

Rusted Wasteland Series:

STEEL GUARDIAN

STEEL DEFENDER

STEEL PROTECTOR

STEEL SIEGE

STEEL SOLDIER

STEEL LEGACY

STEEL APOCALYPSE (*A Robot's Journal*) - free on cameroncoral.com/blockjournal

Cyborg Guardian Chronicles:

STOLEN FUTURE

CODED RED

ORIGIN LOOP

Rogue Spark Series:

ALTERED

BRINK

DORMANT

SALVAGE

AFTER WE FALL (*A Rogue Spark Novel*) - free on CameronCoral.com

Short Stories:

CROSSING THE VOID: *A Space Opera Science-Fiction Short Story*

Acknowledgments

Thank you, dear reader, for picking up the second installment in Block's adventures. I'm guessing you enjoyed *Steel Guardian* enough to continue on, and for that I'm truly grateful.

After my baby niece Hannah was born, I had this idea floating in my head—what if a robot had to care for a baby? Would it know what to do? How would it deal with the situation, especially when faced with a post-apocalyptic, war-ravaged landscape? And thus, the concept for the *Rusted Wasteland* series took root.

Several robots inspired the character of Block: the protective *Lost in Space* robot; the friendly *Johnny 5* from Short Circuit; and the heart-achingly kind WALL-E.

Thanks to J. Thorn and Zach Bohannon for their guidance on *Steel Guardian*. The series would not be so strong without their challenge to make it my very best.

I owe a massive debt of thanks to my editor, Lori Diederich. Once again, she rescued me from grave mistakes and polished the draft into a finished book that makes me proud.

Roy Migabon is the talented artist behind the series covers, and I'm in awe of his vision.

A huge thank you to my incredible Cameron Coral VIP readers! You are supportive, patient, and meticulous in your reading.

I wrote this book during the outbreak of the COVID-19 pandemic while quarantining. My husband, Steve, makes every day brighter and helped guide me in creating Block's world. His spirited encouragement kept me going.

Post-apocalyptic settings can be grim, especially when the real world becomes unpredictable and more dystopian. My intent in creating Block's universe is to offer an escape. To me, there is nothing so special as losing yourself in a story you enjoy.

I remain ever hopeful for our future, the innate goodness in people, and unimaginable technology breakthroughs. Block is the kind of robot that I hope becomes a part of my household someday... and perhaps yours, if you'd like.

Be well,

Cameron Coral
July 2020
Chicago, Illinois

About the Author

Cameron Coral is an award-nominated science fiction author. Her book *Steel Guardian* about a post-apocalyptic CleanerBot placed second in the Self-Published Science Fiction Competition (SPSFC).

Growing up with a NASA engineer in the family instilled a deep respect for science and for asking lots of questions. Watching tons of Star Trek episodes helped, too. Her imagination is fueled by breakthroughs in robotics, space travel, and psychology.

After moving around a lot (Canada, Arizona, Maryland, Australia), she now lives in Northern Illinois with her husband and a "shorty" Jack Russell terrier who runs the house.

Want a free novel, advance copies of books, and occasional rants about why robots are awesome? Visit her website:

CameronCoral.com

instagram.com/cameroncoralauthor

tiktok.com/@cameroncoral

Printed in Great Britain
by Amazon

40719830R00189